MARY ANNE AND TOO MANY BOYS

**Other books by
Ann M. Martin**

Rachel Parker, Kindergarten Show-off
Eleven Kids, One Summer
Ma and Pa Dracula
Yours Turly, Shirley
Ten Kids, No Pets
Slam Book
Just a Summer Romance
Missing Since Monday
With You and Without You
Me and Katie (the Pest)
Stage Fright
Inside Out
Bummer Summer

BABY-SITTERS LITTLE SISTER series
THE BABY-SITTERS CLUB mysteries
THE BABY-SITTERS CLUB series

AR=MG (4.4) 4

G.ft.—Flock Family 8·6∘

Donated by
The Flock Family

*The author gratefully acknowledges
Mary Lou Kennedy
for her help in
preparing this manuscript.*

Cover art by Hodges Soileau

ISBN 0-590-73283-8

12 11 10 9 8 7 6 5 4 3 2   6 7 8 9/9 0 1/0

Printed in the U.S.A.   40

THE BABY-SITTERS Club

MARY ANNE AND TOO MANY BOYS

Ann M. Martin

AN
APPLE
PAPERBACK

SCHOLASTIC INC.
New York Toronto London Auckland Sydney

CHAPTER 1

I was so excited I felt like doing cartwheels across Claudia Kishi's bedroom floor. It was summer (at last!) and my friends and I were gathered for a special meeting of the Baby-sitters Club.

I looked around the room, and it was pretty obvious that my friends were as excited as I was. Of course, everyone was trying *very hard* to be cool, because that's the way our club president, Kristy Thomas, expects us to be.

Even though we were starting our summer vacations, she insisted on business as usual. Kristy was perched in a director's chair, wearing a red T-shirt, faded jeans, and a visor. She glanced at her watch just as our two junior officers, Mallory Pike and Jessi Ramsey, scooted into the room and flopped down on the floor.

"You're late," Kristy said sternly.

Jessi and Mal are younger than the rest of

us (and happen to be best friends) but Kristy believes that rules are rules. She takes her duty as president very seriously and believes that nothing — short of an earthquake — is an excuse for being late. But I can understand why she feels that way. The Baby-sitters Club was her idea, and I can still remember the day she told Claudia and me about it. All of us had grown up together on Bradford Court and loved to baby-sit, but it took someone like Kristy to set the wheels in motion for an actual sitting business.

But back to Mal and Jessi. "Sorry," they murmured in unison. They looked like they were trying hard not to giggle. Mal and Jessi always stick together, and besides, how could anyone take things seriously on the first day of summer?

"I can't believe you're going to California tonight," I whispered to Dawn Schafer. Dawn is my stepsister (her mother married my father), and she was going to the West Coast to visit her father and brother for two weeks.

"I can't believe it, either. It will be so much fun to go home. I mean, to my second home," she added quickly.

Her second home? I guess I should explain that. Even though she lives in Stoneybrook, Connecticut, now, Dawn is a California girl

2

at heart. She loves the sun and the ocean, and is into health food in a major way. She even looks like someone out of a California beach movie. If you've already guessed that she's blonde, blue-eyed, and has the kind of dazzling smile you see in toothpaste commercials — you're right! Besides being my stepsister, Dawn is my "other" best friend. (Kristy Thomas is also my best friend.) There was definitely some jealousy involved when Dawn and I became stepsisters. Kristy seemed hurt that Dawn and I were spending so much time together, and I had to reassure her that it wouldn't affect our friendship.

I just realized I haven't told you who I am, so here's a capsule biography, as my English teacher would say. My name is Mary Anne Spier. I am thirteen years old and an eighth-grader at Stoneybrook Middle School. I don't have a yard of wheat-colored hair like Dawn. Instead, I have brown hair, brown eyes, and think of myself as kind of ordinary. Oh, yes, one more thing. I have a fantastic gray kitten named Tigger.

"Have you said good-bye to Logan?" Dawn asked in a low voice.

"I called him last night."

I knew it would be hard to say good-bye to Logan, so I had decided to get it over with quickly. Logan Bruno is my boyfriend, but I still have a little trouble getting used to the idea. Logan is the cutest boy I have ever seen. He looks just like Cam Geary, my favorite TV star, and he comes from Louisville, Kentucky. He has this smooth southern accent and a voice that makes me think of warm molasses. Logan is an associate member of the BSC, which means he doesn't come to meetings, but he fills in occasionally when all the regular members are busy. (Our other associate member is Shannon Kilbourne, a friend of Kristy's.)

"He's really going to miss you," Dawn said softly. "But I guess the feeling is mutual."

I nodded. Even though I had a wonderful two weeks at Sea City, this fantastic beach in New Jersey, ahead of me, I knew I would miss Logan. A lot.

"Can we please come to order?" Kristy said abruptly. I glanced around the room as the meeting began. It's amazing how many good things have happened for me because of the Baby-sitters Club. Dawn feels the same way. When we became friends, which was right after she moved here from California, I talked the BSC members into letting her join the club. About a year later we became stepsisters. But you're probably wondering how the club got started, and this would be a good time to tell you a little bit about it.

One day Kristy noticed that her mom was having a terrible time trying to find a sitter for David Michael, Kristy's little brother. Kristy couldn't sit for him, and neither could her two older brothers. So Mrs. Thomas was making calls all over town and getting nowhere. Then Kristy had a great idea. Why not form a baby-sitters club to solve that kind of problem?

This is how it works. A group of us meet on Mondays, Wednesdays, and Fridays from 5:30 to 6:00 in Claudia Kishi's bedroom. Why did we pick Claudia's room? Because she has her own phone and her own private number. Anyone who wants a baby-sitter can call us at that time, and they immediately reach seven sitters at once. The idea is perfect — and so simple, we wondered why we hadn't thought of it before.

Kristy is the president, because the club was her idea, and Claudia is the vice-president, since her room is our headquarters. Stacey McGill likes numbers, so she's our treasurer. My stepsister, Dawn, is our official alternate officer. Dawn has to be familiar with the job of every club officer and be able to substitute for anyone who can't make a meeting. She really likes being an alternate because she gets to take on lots of different roles in the club.

Mal and Jessi are junior officers as I mentioned. Since they are eleven years old, they can only baby-sit after school and on weekends, but they are *very* responsible. (They don't have actual club duties, though.) Mal and Jessi have a lot in common. They are both the oldest children in their families, and both of them complain that their parents treat them like babies.

I have the best job of all. (In my opinion.) I am the club secretary, and I keep our record book. The record book lists all our baby-sitting appointments, along with the rates our clients pay, and how much each of us earns at each job. I also have to keep track of each member's schedule — I could tell you when Jessi has a ballet lesson or Kristy has softball practice — and I have never made a scheduling mistake.

I was flipping through the record book when Kristy called on Stacey McGill to give the treasurer's report. Stacey looked very "New York" as usual, in a pair of khaki safari pants, topped with a jungle-print blouse and a leather belt that must have cost two months' allowance. Stacey is a real city girl. She grew up in New York, and when her family moved to Stoneybrook, Claudia became friendly with her and invited her to join the club. Stacey is extremely sophisticated, but she does have her problems. Her parents recently divorced and her father lives in New York. And she has a disease called diabetes, which means she has to stick to a strict no-sweets diet and give herself daily injections of something called insulin.

"Well that's about it," Stacey said, finishing her report. She looked at me and grinned. "Do you realize where we'll be tomorrow at this time?"

"I sure do," I blurted out. "Sea City!"

Kristy frowned. "I know everyone's excited about their vacation plans, but could we *please* keep this meeting going?"

"Sorry about that." I tried to look remorseful, but it was difficult because I know I was still grinning from ear to ear. Stacey McGill and I were going to spend two fantastic weeks at a real beach town, and I couldn't wait to get started! It wasn't exactly a vacation (we were going to be mother's helpers for a family — the Pikes — just like we had done the last time they went to the beach), but it would be wonderful. I was sure of it! I tried to restrain myself, though, because I remembered that Kristy's family hadn't made any vacation plans. Kristy would be in Stoneybrook for the next couple of weeks. Of course some people would say that Kristy is *always* on vacation, because she lives in a house that is straight out of the movies. Kristy used to live next door to me, but when her mother (who was divorced) married a millionaire named Watson Brewer, the whole family moved across town to his mansion. Kristy's family immediately increased in size. Watson has two cute kids who spend every other weekend with him, and recently Kristy's mom and Watson adopted an adorable little Vietnamese girl. She is two years old and her name is Emily.

Kristy nudged me impatiently. "How does the record book look, Mary Anne?" Kristy likes to plan everything days in advance and doesn't like surprises.

"You're going to be busy," I told her, flipping through the calendar pages. "Of course, you'll have Jessi to help you." (Jessi didn't have any vacation plans, either.)

Jessi is a really neat black girl who moved to Stoneybrook from Oakley, New Jersey. She's in the sixth grade (like Mallory), and is a very talented ballet dancer. She has an eight-year-old sister named Becca, and a baby brother nicknamed Squirt. Jessi can handle almost any situation, and proved it once by pet-sitting for a houseful of animals for a week.

"It looks like you both have interesting jobs lined up," I went on.

Jessi beamed. "I'm sitting for Charlotte Johanssen one afternoon." Charlotte is one of our favorite kids.

"I'm sitting for Jenny Prezzioso," Kristy said glumly.

Jenny Prezzioso. Everybody was silent for a moment while the name sank in. Jenny is the kind of kid who gives baby-sitting a bad name, although I guess it isn't really her fault. She's only four years old, but she's headed for the "World's Most Spoiled Kid" award.

"You'll be able to handle her," Claudia said cheerfully. "Just don't let her eat pizza if she's wearing one of her Little Bo-Peep dresses."

"Pizza!" Mal exclaimed. "I wish you hadn't said that. I'm starving!" As soon as the words were out of her mouth, her stomach gave a loud growl, just like a sound effect in a movie. "Oh, how awful." She clutched her stomach in embarrassment and giggled.

Claudia reached under the bed and pulled out a shoe box. "Help yourself." The box tipped open and I could see it was filled with Twinkies, Gummy Bears, and M&M's.

Nobody thought it was odd that Claudia kept snacks under the bed. Claudia is a junk-food addict, and she has candy and cookies stashed all over her room. Her parents aren't thrilled about it, so she keeps her "treats" safely tucked away. Claudia, by the way, is definitely the most dramatic-looking person in the club. She's Japanese-American, and has long black hair and almond-shaped eyes. She's a great artist and has an incredibly brainy sister, Janine. (Claudia is *not* the world's best student, so it's just as well that she's talented in other areas.)

"Mary Anne," Stacey said dreamily, "remember the pizza at Sea City?"

"How could I forget?" I sighed happily. "Even pepperoni tastes better in Sea City." When Stacey and I had been to Sea City with the Pikes before, we'd had a super time. If you like to eat, you would go crazy at Sea City, because you can find everything from banana fudge to foot-long hot dogs there.

"And Burger Garden," Stacey went on. "Remember those Crazy Burgers?"

"Of course I do," I said. "Burgers topped with bacon, Swiss cheese, pickles, and orange sauce."

"Orange sauce? Yuck!" Jessi looked slightly sick.

"It's not what you think," I told her. "They just mix the ketchup and mustard together.

The Pike kids love it, don't you, Mal?"

"We sure do." Mal nodded enthusiastically. Mallory is the oldest of *eight* kids, so naturally she is a terrific baby-sitter. The last time she went to Sea City she was a little young to baby-sit, so Stacey and I had all the responsibility for her brothers and sisters. Now that Mal is older, her parents have decided to pay her to help us out. But just from time to time. For the most part, they want her to have fun and enjoy her vacation.

Every year Mal's family rents a big house at the beach, and the kids love it. Stoneybrook is on the water, but it isn't the same thing. It isn't a "beach town" the way Sea City is. There must be a million things to do in Sea City, and I don't mean just the ocean and the boardwalk.

"Remember how much fun we had at Trampoline Land?" Stacey said.

"And Fred's Putt-Putt Course!" Mal exclaimed. "I love miniature golf. And the Ferris wheel, and oh, Candy Kitchen and Ice-Cream Palace!"

Kristy looked a little put out by this trip down memory lane, so I decided to change the subject.

"How about you, Claudia? Are you all set for Vermont?"

"I think so," she said softly. She looked a

little wistful and I knew she was thinking of Mimi, her grandmother. Mimi died recently, and this year's vacation in the mountains just wouldn't be the same without her. The Kishis were even going to a different spot, because it would be too painful to go back to the old place.

"I suppose we can close the meeting now," Kristy said reluctantly. I know she was disappointed that most of us were taking off for exciting places, while she and Jessi would be stuck at home in Stoneybrook.

"Gosh, I'm going to miss everybody," I said suddenly. It had just dawned on me that I wouldn't see my friends for two whole weeks!

Before I had a chance to get misty-eyed (I cry *very* easily), Kristy thumped me on the shoulder. "Hey, don't turn on the waterworks. We're all going to write each other!"

"That's true," I said, trying to cheer up, "but it won't be the same." I could feel a lump rising in my throat and swallowed hard. "I'll send everybody tons of postcards. And make sure you write me back," I pleaded. (We had already exchanged addresses.)

"Of course we will," Jessi promised. "Kristy and I will tell you about our baby-sitting jobs."

"And we'll write everything in the club notebook," Kristy said. (The club notebook is like a diary. We write up what happens on every job we go to. Leave it to Kristy to be businesslike at a time like this.)

I hate good-byes, so I didn't object when Stacey pulled me toward the hallway. "Have a great time, everybody!" she yelled over her shoulder. Dawn and Mallory were already ahead of us, thundering down the stairs, eager to start their vacations. Kristy and Jessi looked a little sad standing in Claudia's bedroom, and I could feel myself getting weepy again.

"Come on, Mary Anne!" Stacey exclaimed. "Sea City is waiting for us."

She was right. I wiped away a tear that was threatening to trickle down my cheek. Who could cry when it was vacation time?

CHAPTER 2

"Which do you like better? The pink or the blue?"

Dawn snatched up identical bikinis from her dresser drawer and waved them at me.

"Um . . . I like them both," I said.

"Honestly, Mary Anne! You must like one a teeny bit more than the other." She collapsed on the bed next to her open suitcase. It was late Friday afternoon, and her bedroom looked like a tornado had just ripped through. Dawn was packing for California, and every single surface was littered with clothes. She could have held a rummage sale. When our parents got married, we started out as roommates, but it was a disaster, and we decided on separate rooms. I glanced at the piles of clothes scattered around and remembered why.

"You look great in pink *and* blue," I said defensively. "I wasn't just being polite. Anyway, why don't you bring both of them? You

14

can always use an extra suit at the beach."

Dawn started to laugh. "An extra suit!" she said, sitting up and drawing her knees to her chin. "I'm bringing *six* bathing suits with me — three bikinis and three tank suits."

"Oh," I said, feeling a little silly. Dawn really dresses like an "individual," and to her, a bathing suit is more than something to swim in. It's a fashion statement.

"Hey, I just thought of something," she said. "I've got a string bikini that would look great on you. It's one of those green metallic ones. You know, the kind that always looks wet?"

"No thanks," I said quickly. "I'm all set." I could just picture what my father would do if he thought I was packing a string bikini for Sea City! Even though Dad has mellowed a lot in the last few months, he's still pretty conservative. It's hard to believe, but in the old days, I had so many rules, I felt like I was in boot camp. I had to be home by nine, I had to wear my hair in pigtails, and worst of all, my father picked out my *clothes* for me. I think part of the reason is that my mother died when I was little, and Dad had to be a mother *and* a father to me. Luckily, he has loosened up a lot, even though he will never be as casual about things as Sharon (Dawn's mom) is.

I was Dawn's first friend when she moved to Stoneybrook after her parents got divorced. We got along great from day one. You can imagine how surprised we were when we discovered that her mom and my dad went to high school together, and that they'd even gone *steady*. Their story is very romantic (and a little sad) because although they'd loved each other, they'd broken up. Why? Because Dawn's grandparents didn't approve of my father! Anyway, years later, when Sharon and my dad met each other again, they realized that they still were in love and finally decided to get married. All of us moved into Dawn's house, and although things were a little rocky at first, everyone is happy now.

"Mary Anne, I have some suntan lotion for you." Dad tapped on the open bedroom door and then came in, followed by Sharon.

"Thanks, Dad, but I've got tons of sunblock." I learned my lesson the last time I went to Sea City and ended up looking like a lobster. For some reason, I am one of those people who *never* tan. I just go directly from dead white to flaming red, followed by some painful peeling.

"How about toothpaste, shampoo, and stationery?" Dawn's mom asked. She fumbled in the pocket of her pink jumpsuit, looking a little distracted. "And I bought each of you a roll of stamps, but what in the world did I do with them?"

It's really funny when Sharon tries to be organized and in control, because she's the most disorganized person I've ever met. If you don't believe me, you should see our kitchen. Last week, I found the grocery list (with a pencil still attached) in the refrigerator, and a very ripe tomato in the coupon drawer. I couldn't tell you how they got there, and I bet Sharon couldn't, either.

"Oh, dear," she said, searching in her pocket again. "Would you believe I actually made a list of what you both would need for two weeks?" I'd believe it. Sharon is a great list-maker. The trouble is she always loses a list five minutes after she writes it.

"Don't worry, Mom," Dawn said reassuringly. "I'm ready to go. I just have to throw in a beach cover-up and a hair dryer, and then I'll be all packed."

"It's true," I said, catching Dad's worried glance. "The room just *looks* like a disaster. She's really in good shape."

"You could have fooled me," Dad said, shaking his head.

One of the reason's Dawn's room looked so cluttered is that it is very small. All the rooms in Dawn's house are small, because that was the style back then. I should explain that when Dawn's mother moved to Stoneybrook from California after her divorce last year, she bought a house for herself, Dawn, and Jeff. (Jeff is Dawn's younger brother.) But not just any house — a farmhouse that is so old it's practically an historic landmark. It was built in 1795, and has an outhouse, a barn, and an old smokehouse. It looks like a large, creepy dollhouse, the kind of place that a ghost would love to call home. (And probably does!) Dawn and her mom are crazy over it. Jeff, her brother, wasn't crazy over *anything* in Stoneybrook, though, so he eventually moved back to California to be with his dad.

But back to Dawn, who was sitting on her suitcase to close it. "I think that about does it," she said, looking a little flushed with the effort. Dawn was dressed for traveling, which meant she was wearing a beautiful Laura Ashley dress and had swept her long blonde hair back in pearl barrettes.

"Then let's have a quick dinner and be off to the airport," Sharon said. "I made something special for your last meal here, Dawn," she added, heading for the door.

Dad and I exchanged a look. Neither one of

us likes health food as much as Sharon and Dawn do.

"Something special?" I ventured. I was *starving* and hoped she hadn't made one of her famous tofu casseroles.

"Something you *both* like," Sharon said, stopping to put an arm around me. "Spinach lasagna, tossed salad, and Italian bread."

"That sounds great!" I breathed a sigh of relief.

"And for dessert," she went on, "Tofu Delight!"

It was nearly seven o'clock when we got to the airport, and I could tell Dawn was feeling a little nervous about her flight to California. She checked her purse three times to make sure she had her ticket, while the four of us strolled up and down the long concourse.

"Did you bring some snacks for the trip?" I asked her.

"Of course." Dawn grinned and patted her carryon bag. "An apple, some dates, and two granola bars. Plus they give you something to eat on the plane."

"Something cardboard," Sharon said crisply.

"No," Dawn laughed. "Something edible. I

checked." She paused and looked at me. "I left that new mystery book on your dresser for you to read. And if you want to take any of my tapes to Sea City, they're in the shoe box in my closet."

I smiled. Dawn and I don't usually have the same taste in music, but it was a nice thought. "Thanks," I said slowly. I was surprised to find that my voice was a little quavery. It was crazy, but I was already starting to miss Dawn.

Maybe she felt the same way, because she looked at me very seriously. "I wish you were coming with me, Mary Anne. You'd love California."

I shrugged. "I'll have my hands full with all those Pike kids in Sea City."

She smiled. "I know, but remember not to work all the time. Take some time out to have fun."

Dawn's flight was announced then, and Sharon enveloped Dawn in a big hug. "Are you *sure* you have everything?" she asked for the dozenth time. "Tickets, money . . ."

"Everything, Mom," Dawn told her. They looked amazingly alike. Blonde, blue-eyed, and pretty.

Dad hugged Dawn then, even though I think he felt shy about doing it. Dad always feels a little uncomfortable around kids, probably because I am his only child and the two of us lived alone for so many years.

Dawn turned to me with her arms outstretched, and the tears welled up in my eyes. "Oh, Dawn, I'm really going to miss you!" I blurted out.

"Me, too," she said awkwardly, patting my back. "I just hate good-byes." She pulled away to look at me and I saw that her eyes were misty. "Don't make me cry, okay? I can't get on that plane with mascara dribbling down my cheeks!"

"Okay," I said, sniffling a little. I was trying hard to be brave, but deep down, I felt like bawling. I couldn't believe I was losing my stepsister for two whole weeks.

"Send lots of postcards!" Dawn called as she headed toward the gate. "And tell me *everything!*"

"I will," I promised. I dabbed at my eyes with a tissue.

"She'll be back before you know it," Dad said consolingly.

I nodded, afraid I would start crying again. Suddenly two weeks seemed like two years.

It was impossible to sleep that night. I tossed and turned, thumped the pillow, and tried to imagine what Dawn would do when she reached California. I pictured her having lemonade with Jeff and her father. Maybe they were relaxing outside on a big wraparound deck. Dawn told me her father has a really cool house with terra-cotta floors and skylights in almost all the rooms. Plus they have a housekeeper, so she doesn't have to worry about kitchen duty.

Then I started thinking about my trip to Sea City in the morning. I went through a checklist of everything I needed to take. And *then* I started thinking of all the things the Pikes would need to take for eight kids. Try to imagine it. Pails, shovels, beach blankets, and bathing suits, plus tons of rainy-day toys for kids of all different ages. Just thinking about it must have made me tired, because the next thing I knew, I had buried my face in my pillow and fallen sound asleep.

"Mary Anne, we're going to be late!"

"I'm coming, Dad. Just one more hug." I crouched down so Tigger and I were on eye level (he was stretched out on the sofa) and kissed the top of his head. I couldn't stand to say good-bye to him.

"We'll take good care of him," Sharon promised.

"I know you will." Sharon isn't exactly a cat fan, but I think Tigger is growing on her.

After I hugged Sharon good-bye, Dad dropped me off at the Pikes'. Yow, *another* good-bye, I thought as he set my gear on their driveway.

"Take care of yourself, honey," Dad said. I wasn't sure, but I thought he hugged me extra tightly, since I was going to be gone for a long time. I got through this last good-bye pretty easily, though, because Claire, Margo, and Nicky Pike all came barreling out of the garage, carrying suitcases.

"Come on, Mary Anne-silly-billy-goo-goo," Claire said. "It's time to go!" Claire is the youngest Pike and is going through an incredibly silly stage.

I helped load both cars (the Pikes always take two station wagons to Sea City) and at the very last minute, Stacey arrived with her mother. Stacey's mother looked a little sad and I knew she was going to miss her. Stacey is her only child, just like I'm Dad's only child. But Mrs. McGill would be alone for the next two weeks, while my dad would have Sharon and Tigger.

We finally straightened out who was going in which car. (I was going with Mrs. Pike,

23

Vanessa, and the triplets, and Stacey was going with Mr. Pike, Mallory, Claire, Margo, and Nicky.)

We were just pulling out of the driveway when Vanessa yelled, "Wait a minute. We forgot Frodo!"

Mrs. Pike turned around to smile at her. Frodo is the Pikes' pet hamster. "Vanessa, Jessi's taking care of him at her house, remember?" Jessi has a hamster of her own named Misty, so she'd know how to look after Frodo.

"Oh, yeah." Vanessa settled back, sighing with relief.

"Now if there are no more problems, it's — "

Right on cue, the triplets sprang to life. "Sea City, here we come!"

CHAPTER 3

Saturday

Hi, Kristy!
    We made it to Sea City, but I feel like I've been through some sort of natural disaster — maybe an earthquake or a hurricane. I guess that's what a car trip with a bunch of kids does to you. Vanessa recited poetry nonstop, the triplets staged a running battle with Nicky, who rode in Stacey's car, and Claire gave us all the scare of our lives. I have no idea what will happen next!
    More later, MaryAnne

Do you know exactly how many words rhyme with cat? I do. Vanessa used every single one of them during our trip to the beach. Vanessa is nine years old and wants to be a poet. I should say, she *is* a poet, because she is always making up poems. And you know what? It must be contagious, because now I find myself doing the same thing when I'm around her!

We were only a few miles out of Stoneybrook when it started. Vanessa and I were riding in the front seat with Mrs. Pike, and the triplets were bouncing around in the back. The triplets, in case you don't know, are named Adam, Jordan, and Byron, and they are ten years old.

"Can we stop for donuts?" Adam yelled. "There's a place right up ahead."

"Certainly not," Mrs. Pike said. "We'll stop at Howard Johnson's at the halfway point like we always do."

"Oh, Mom . . ." Adam whined. "We're starving."

"Adam, don't be a pest. It's all for the best." Vanessa looked very pleased with herself.

Oh, no. Here we go, I thought. "Come on, Adam. You can hold out for another hour or so," I said encouragingly.

"That's right," Vanessa went on. "It's a very short ride, and you'll soon see the tide." Jordan stuck his fingers in his ears, but she ignored him. "A day at the beach is like a fresh peach. A trip to the shore leaves you begging for more. A drive to the ocean is like a . . ." she paused, temporarily stumped.

"Mom!" Byron screeched. "Make her stop that. She's driving me crazy!"

Mrs. Pike just smiled and shook her head. I should tell you that the Pikes have very liberal ideas about raising kids. (Totally opposite from my father's ideas.) The Pike kids are allowed to do pretty much what they want, within reason. They don't have to eat foods they don't like, and they can stay up as late as they want, as long as they're in bed. Mrs. Pike would *never* tell Vanessa to stop making up poems because she thinks that kids should be allowed to express themselves.

"Vanessa," I said gently, "you picked a bad *time* to make up a — " I nearly said *"rhyme,"* but luckily I stopped myself.

"Make up a what?" she asked with a knowing smile.

"A . . . a poem."

She shrugged. "But there's nothing to do." I braced myself for what was coming. "And you know that it's true."

27

"Vanessa," Jordan said warningly from the backseat.

I thought fast. "I know. We'll all play a game — "

"But it won't be the same." Vanessa grinned.

I sighed. I could see it was a losing battle.

"Hey, I've got one," Adam shouted. "How's this? We're stuck in the car, and the ocean is far."

Vanessa turned around and stuck out her tongue at him. I don't think she liked being upstaged by her brother.

"Hah! You're a poet, and you didn't know it!" Jordan chimed in.

I was about to suggest a game of I Spy when Mr. Pike suddenly pulled up next to us on the three-lane highway.

"There's Daddy!" Vanessa shrieked. Mr. Pike tooted the horn, and Nicky, who is eight, pulled out his cheeks and made a really disgusting face against the window.

"Yuck!" Jordan yelled as Mr. Pike sped away. "Let's get him back!"

"Darn. It's too late now, but if we hurry up we can get him next time." Adam reached for a pad of construction paper I had tucked into a tote bag. "Quick! Anybody got a Magic Marker?"

Byron grinned. "Write something really gross!" he said, fumbling in a box of toys and art materials for rainy days.

"Um, I'm not sure this is a good idea," I began. I felt I *had* to speak up, since Mrs. Pike was humming along with a song on the radio and watching the road. She didn't seem the least bit worried that the triplets were planning a major war!

Adam frowned, waiting for inspiration to strike. Then he smiled, just like Road Runner plotting some awful revenge, and wrote: Batman has a Bird Brain.

Batman has a Bird Brain? I turned around to stare at Adam. "I don't get it," I said. I noticed that Mrs. Pike was gaining on Mr. Pike, and the two cars would be side by side in just a minute.

Adam hooted. "Nicky is *so* proud of his new Batman T-shirt, he's been wearing it day and night."

"Yeah, he bought it with his own money, and he thinks he's really cool," Byron piped up.

"He won't think he's so cool when he sees your sign," Jordan said happily.

Jordan was right. Nicky was furious. He stared at the sign, glanced down at his shirt, and turned beet-red. He shook his fist at us, just as our car suddenly changed lanes and charged ahead of them.

The triplets were practically rolling off the seats with laughter as I racked my brain, trying to think of something to do to distract them. For the next few minutes, they turned down every single car game I could think of. I guess "Get Your Brother" was more fun.

They held up the Batman sign about five more times during the next hour — every time the two cars came side by side. Nicky was so mad, I expected to see smoke coming out of his ears!

At last we reached the halfway point. "This is it," Mrs. Pike said cheerfully.

I have never been so glad to see a Howard Johnson's in my life. Everyone piled out of the car, and after a quick trip to the restrooms, we all met at the take-out counter. Mallory and Stacey were ordering ice-cream cones for Claire and Margo, while Nicky was struggling to make up his mind.

"Get Cherries Jubilee," Mal suggested. "Or Rocky Road."

"Don't get Rum Raisin," Margo said. "It looks like vanilla ice cream with flies."

Stacey and I led the kids to a small picnic area while Mr. and Mrs. Pike sat at the counter and ordered coffee. Stacey was the only one of us without an ice-cream cone — because of her diabetes — so she was munching on an apple.

"Tough trip," she said, and sighed. "It's a good thing Nicky was in a separate car from the triplets or it would have been World War Three."

I nodded. For some reason Nicky and the triplets manage to fight over *everything*, and I noticed that Nicky was sitting as far away from them as possible.

"How's your Pistachio Crunch?" Stacey asked me.

"Fantastic." I used to feel guilty about eating ice cream and candy in front of Stacey, but she handles her diabetes so well, I hardly think about it anymore.

Mr. and Mrs. Pike wandered out with the remains of their coffee then, and joined Mal and the triplets at one of the long wooden picnic tables.

Stacey sat on the grass and turned her face up to the sun. A few people glanced over at us curiously, probably wondering if we were part of the huge Pike family. I scanned the two picnic tables then, and something seemed out of place. What was wrong?

I did a quick head count. And came up with eleven. *Eleven?* There should be twelve of us.

The eight Pike kids, Mr. and Mrs. Pike, Stacey and me.

"Ohmigosh," I muttered under my breath.

"What's up?" Stacey asked lazily. She was stretched out like a cat, enjoying the warm sun.

"Stacey," I said, not taking my eyes off the kids, "we're missing somebody."

She sat up fast. "Are you sure?" She did her own head count, without waiting for my answer.

"I'm sure." I gulped. "There are the triplets and Mal and Vanessa and Nicky and Margo." And no Claire, I added silently.

"Where's Claire?" Mrs. Pike said loudly.

"I was just wondering the same thing," I said, as Stacey scrambled to her feet. "Have you kids seen her?" The triplets solemnly shook their heads, and Mrs. Pike glanced nervously at the parking lot.

"Maybe she went back to the car," she said a little breathlessly. I know she was really worried, even though she was trying not to show it.

Mr. Pike stood up. "I'll check the car. Stacey, why don't you look around the play area." (There were a couple of swing sets at the far side of the parking lot.)

"I'll go back inside," I said suddenly.

"Maybe she had to go to the bathroom."

Mr. Pike nodded and hurried off, his expression tense. Claire is only five years old, and at that age, kids shouldn't be out of your sight for even a minute.

I quickly checked the restroom, the water fountain, and the phone booth. No sign of her. I was about to dash outside when I spotted her at the counter, happily spinning on a stool.

"Claire!" I said, rushing up to her. "We thought you were missing." I hugged her, my heart still doing flip-flops in my chest.

"I'm not missing," she said seriously. "I'm right here. All my ice cream leaked out, so I came back to get another cone." She held up an empty cone. The bottom was jagged as if she had bitten it off.

"We can fix that," a boy behind the counter said. "What kind of ice cream did you have?"

"Vanilla. I always get vanilla."

He handed her a new cone and winked. "Make sure you eat this one from the top down, not the bottom up."

We hurried outside, just as Mr. and Mrs. Pike were coming through the glass double doors. They swept Claire into their arms and hugged her, just like I had done.

We piled back in the cars, and after endless rhyming, Vanessa shrieked with joy.

"There's the cow sign!" she said, jabbing me in the ribs and forgetting to make a poem. The cow sign is one of the Pike kids' favorite landmarks. It's a billboard with a three-dimensional purple cow, and they look for it every year.

"And there's Crabs for Grabs!" Jordan yelled a few minutes later. Crabs for Grabs is a seafood restaurant on the outskirts of Sea City.

"And the suntan girl!" Adam and Byron shouted together. The suntan girl is *another* billboard that they always watch for. "And *there* is Sea City!"

We're finally here, I thought. I started to relax and then caught myself. Who knew what would happen next!

CHAPTER 4

Saturday

Dear Dawn,
    I'd have to write a book to tell you all about the trip down here, so I'll just say it was an adventure. The Pike kids are really excited to be back in Sea City, and so am I. Even though I miss all of you (and a certain person with the initials L.B.) I think I'm in for a very interesting two weeks, and I want to trade stories the minute you get back. I bet you're tan already!
                    Bye for now,
                    Mary Anne

"The wind chimes are still here!" Jordan shouted.

"And they left the swing up!" Adam said, throwing himself into a white wicker swing on the front porch.

"The honeysuckle bush is blooming, just like before," Vanessa said dreamily. She buried her face in the soft blossoms for a moment.

"Okay, gang," Mr. Pike said firmly. "I know you want to run around and look at everything, but what do we have to do first?"

"Unpack?" Nicky suggested.

Mr. Pike nodded, and there was a chorus of groans.

I took a deep breath of salty air while Mrs. Pike unlocked the front door of the house. The Pikes rent the same place every year, and it looks like something out of Hansel and Gretel. It's a giant gingerbread house, which Mrs. Pike says is Victorian style. It's painted yellow with white trim, and has carved railings and posts and eaves and edges. Best of all, it has a big front porch, so you can sit for hours and look at the ocean (if you're not busy running after eight kids). The Pikes love it because they have the beach right in their own front yard.

After we helped unload the car, Stacey and

I headed upstairs for the yellow bedroom we'd shared the last time. It's very old-fashioned (maybe a little too much for Stacey) and has two high, dark wood beds, a bare wood floor, and yellow flowered wallpaper. It also has a great view of the ocean, and I stood and watched the sun glittering on the water for a moment before I tackled my suitcase. I saw a lifeguard talking to some little kids splashing in the surf, and I thought of a lifeguard we met here the last time. His name was Scott, and Stacey had an *incredible* crush on him. Unfortunately he was much too old for her (I tried to tell her so at the time), and besides that, he was interested in another girl.

She must have read my mind because she joined me at the window, eyeing the little group on the shore. She watched them for a minute and then said softly, "Thank goodness I'm more grown up this time."

I knew exactly what she meant. "You have to admit it was an interesting vacation."

"Interesting!" Stacey hooted. She curled up on the bed, her knees tucked under her chin. "I can't *believe* I made such an idiot of myself over Scott." She paused, inspecting a frosted-pink fingernail. "Of course, it wasn't a total loss. You met Alex and I met Toby."

"That's right." I sat down next to her. "Do you think they ever think about us?"

Stacey twisted a lock of blonde hair around her finger and frowned. "Probably just once in a while. Toby was really cute, wasn't he?"

I nodded. Toby was one of those totally cool boys (really Stacey's type), but I preferred Alex. Alex was the first mother's helper I ever met who was a *guy!* Alex was great with kids, and we hit it off right from the start.

"Whatever happened to that ring he gave you?" Alex and I exchanged rings on our last night in Sea City, but it didn't mean there was anything really serious between us. (Plus, I didn't know Logan then.) We found this place where you can buy rings and have stuff engraved on them for five dollars each. Alex has a ring with my initials and I have one with his.

"Um, I'm not sure. It's either in the bottom of my dresser drawer, or in a shoe box in my closet."

Stacey pretended to be shocked. "I thought you slept with it under your pillow every night."

I knew she was just teasing. I don't even think of Alex in a romantic way, especially since I've met Logan. I guess Alex played an important part in my life, though, because he was the first boy I was ever interested in.

"Wouldn't it be funny if Alex and Toby showed up again?"

I didn't get a chance to answer because Claire bolted into the room just then and wrapped herself around my knees.

"Can we go to the beach, please, please, please, Mary Anne-silly-billy-goo-goo?"

"We have to finish unpacking," I told her, and Claire's mouth turned down, just like one of those Greek masks that are supposed to stand for "tragedy."

Then she brightened. "What if I help?" she asked. She picked up one of my T-shirts and held it up to her chest. It hung all the way down to her knees.

"The best way you can help is to go back to your own room and get Mal to help you find your bathing suit and beach towel. Then when you're all dressed — and your suitcase is unpacked — we'll hit the beach," I said.

"Promise?"

"Promise." That seemed to satisfy her because she gave a wild whoop of joy and dashed down the hall.

I probably should explain about the sleeping arrangements. Claire and Margo bunk together, Vanessa and Mallory share a pink bedroom, and Stacey and I have the yellow bedroom. The boys have a big bedroom at the end of the hall. There are plenty of rooms to go around, and there is even an extra room with a window seat up on the third floor. It's one of my favorite places to curl up (Mal's, too), and once she and I went up there to watch a lightning storm. Very exciting!

It took at least half an hour to unpack, because Stacey and I kept reminding each other of funny things that happened with Alex, Toby, and Scott, the lifeguard. Actually, the incident with Scott wasn't exactly *funny* (Stacey saw him kissing another girl and dissolved into tears), but I was pretty sure that she was over him.

"How will you feel if you run into Scott on the beach?" I asked her.

"I don't know, but I sure won't rush out and buy any more chocolates." She laughed, and I knew everything would be okay. She had actually bought Scott a ten-dollar box of candy as a going-away present, right before we saw him kissing his girlfriend. Talk about bad timing!

Mal stuck her head in the door just as I was putting the finishing touches on my beach getup.

She stared at me, and her jaw dropped open. "Gosh, Mary Anne," she said, "you look like you're going to the desert."

As I've said, I burn *very* easily, so I have to cover every square inch of myself with sunblock — even on cloudy days.

"This is my beach cover-up, if you'll remember," I said, feeling a little defensive. I was wearing my white caftan that flows around me like a tent. And just to make sure that no rays would sneak in, I put on giant black sunglasses, a straw hat, and covered my nose with sunblock.

Stacey and Mal exchanged a look, and I know they were trying not to burst out laughing. "Are you sure you need all that?" Stacey said, trying to be tactful. "It's pretty late in the day to get burned."

I glanced at myself in the mirror. I *did* look a little strange, but I didn't dare take any chances.

"I'm ready, Mary Anne-silly-billy-goo-goo!" Claire shrieked. She was dressed in a bright red tank suit and wriggling with joy like a puppy.

"Okay, let's go," I said, scooping her up. We met the triplets and Margo in the hall, and I automatically counted heads as we went down the stairs. "Where's Vanessa?" I asked.

(After the scare with Claire, I wasn't taking *any* chances.)

"I'm out here," she called from the front porch. Vanessa was curled up in a wicker chair, balancing a notebook on her knees. She had a dreamy expression on her face, like she was lost in thought.

"Beach time!" I said, ruffling her hair as we went by.

She gave a little smile. "I'll be there in a few minutes," she said. "I have something I want to finish."

Stacey raised her eyebrows. Vanessa is usually the first one to plunge into the waves and never complains even when the water is freezing.

"I'll catch up with you later. Honest." She obviously wanted to be by herself.

"Okay," I said doubtfully, "but don't wait too long or the sun will go down."

"Where does it go?" Claire asked, grabbing my hand and dragging me toward the beach.

I was still watching Vanessa, wondering if something was wrong. "Where does what go?"

"The sun!" She rolled her eyes. "Where does it go when it goes down?"

"Oh." I was stumped.

"Behind a cloud?" Stacey suggested.

"Good answer," I said, just like they say on a TV game show.

Stacey grinned at the compliment. "Any time," she told me.

CHAPTER 5

Sunday

Dear Logan,

Sea City is fantastic!
The beach is great (even
though I am wrapped
up like a mummy to
avoid the sun). The
weather is perfect and
all the kids are getting
along with each other.
I think this is going
to be the best vacation
ever. You would really
love it here! How are
things in Stoneybrook?
If you see Tigger sitting

*in the front window,
be sure to wave to him.
I miss you!*
*Lots of OOO's and xx's,
Mary Anne*

You wouldn't believe how many times I re-
wrote my postcard to Logan. You'd think I
was doing a term paper for Advanced Com-
position class. Of course, it was a lot harder
to write than a term paper, because I had to
find the perfect "tone," as my English teacher
would say. I had to be funny (I thought the
part about the mummy was pretty good), and
I had to sound like I was having a wonderful
time. Of course, I wanted Logan to know that
I would be having an even *better* time if he
were there with me. You see what a problem
I had. I didn't want Logan to think I was pin-
ing away for him, but I also didn't want him
to think I was so super-cool, I didn't even miss
him. What a dilemma! (Another expression my
English teacher uses a lot.)

I tucked the postcard in the bottom of my
underwear drawer before I went to bed Saturday night. When I woke up Sunday morning, I discovered that everything I had said
about the weather had been totally wrong.

45

There was *no* sunshine, and the sea looked grim and choppy. The sky was a flat gray color, like someone had gone over it with a gallon of semigloss paint and a roller. I thought it looked very depressing, although I know that some people don't mind cool, windy days at the beach.

Breakfast was hectic as usual. Mr. Pike was flipping pancakes in what looked like the world's largest frying pan, while Mal was busily making gallons of orange juice. Vanessa buttered a mountain of raisin-bread toast while I microwaved the bacon. Stacey put the triplets to work setting the table, watching to make sure that everybody got the right amount of silverware. You'd be surprised how much planning goes into breakfast for twelve people. Luckily, Mrs. Pike is very organized (unlike my stepmother) and had everything pretty much under control.

"I think it's going to be cloudy all morning," Mrs. Pike said, looking at the overcast sky. "What do you kids want to do today?"

"The beach!" Adam shouted. "What else?" He was polishing off a stack of pancakes at record speed. I noticed he was dressed in his bathing suit, ready to go.

"Not the beach," Mal wailed. "There's no sun today."

"Who cares?" asked Vanessa.

"I do. I want to get a tan." Mal grinned at Stacey and me. "Maybe I'll find a cute guy to impress."

"Only girls care about silly stuff like tanning," Jordan said. He was practically inhaling a bacon sandwich, fidgeting in his chair. "We're going snorkeling today. Right, guys?" He was holding a pair of goggles and a plastic breathing tube on his lap.

"We are?" Nicky said hopefully.

"I meant Adam and Byron," Jordan told him breezily. "You can do something with Margo and Claire. Maybe you could go into town."

Nicky looked crushed. "Oh."

"That's right," Vanessa said brightly. "We can divide up into two groups and that way everyone can do what they want. Will you take us into Sea City, Mary Anne?"

I glanced at Mrs. Pike, and she nodded. "Sure, if Stacey will take the boys swimming."

Mal and the girls and I set out half an hour later (after we persuaded the triplets to let Nicky join them on the beach). Mrs. Pike needed a few things from the grocery store, so we decided to make that our last stop. We walked along the main drag, watching out for familiar landmarks.

"Look, Gurber Garden," Claire shrieked.

"My most favorite place in the whole world."

"Gurber Garden" is really Burger Garden, the place with the Crazy Burgers. (Claire never gets the name right.) It's a fun place to eat. You sit on seats that look like mushrooms and the waiters and waitresses dress up like friendly animals. Who could resist a place where a mouse serves you dinner?

"I thought Ice-Cream Palace was your most favorite place in the world," Mal said, teasing her.

Claire thought about it for a moment. "Can I have two most favorite places?"

"I don't see why not."

It took over an hour to see all the familiar spots. We stopped at Candy Kitchen, and watched while they slid a tray of marshmallow fudge out of the oven. The smell of chocolate was so delicious, we nearly *fainted*, but we decided to save our money for Ice-Cream Palace.

After we took a quick look at Fred's Putt-Putt Course and Hercules' Hot Dogs (the home of the foot-long hot dog), we ended up outside a souvenir shop. There were rows of Sea City T-shirts and shelves filled with mugs, sun visors, straw hats, and beach towels. Everything in the whole store had "Sea City" plastered over it — usually several times. I would have liked to look at the postcards, but I knew the kids were restless.

"What next?" Mal asked. She knew her sisters were getting restless, too.

"Well, we can either walk over to the arcade, or we can save that for another day and head to — " I started to say.

"Ice-Cream Palace!" Claire and Margo yelled.

"Ice-Cream Palace!" Vanessa said, jabbing the air with her fist like a drum major.

"Ice-Cream Palace then," Mal said authoritatively.

I'm not really sure if Ice-Cream Palace has the best ice cream in the world, but it certainly seems that way. Maybe it's just because they have flavors you can't find in Stoneybrook. Sometimes they go a little *too* far trying to be different. (Would you really want to eat something called Banana Bubble-Gum?) But most of their stuff is great.

It always takes the younger kids forever to make up their minds, so we hung over the counter for ages. I decided on two scoops of Rocky Road Delight, since it has all my favorite things — chocolate, marshmallow, and peanuts. Mal chose a strawberry sundae right away. But Margo, Vanessa, and Claire hemmed and hawed for about ten minutes before they could say what they wanted — a chocolate soda for Claire, and hot-fudge sundaes for Margo and Vanessa.

Meanwhile, I saw a cute boy behind the counter eyeing either Mal or Vanessa, sneaking a look every now and then as he put together my cone. He was about twelve, with dark eyes and curly black hair, and I noticed that Vanessa was eyeing him *back*. At least I think she was, although Vanessa has been acting so spacey lately, it's hard to know what she's up to. Sometimes her eyes get this hazy, unfocused look, and she's not really watching anything — she's just writing poetry in her head.

Later, when he leaned across the counter to hand Claire her chocolate soda, I saw that his name tag read "Chris."

"Yummy," Claire said, reaching for the soda. Then it happened. One moment she was clutching the soda in two hands and the next moment she was swimming in chocolate.

"Oh, no," she moaned, looking at her shorts and T-shirt.

"Don't worry," Mal said, reaching for a roll of paper towels. "It will come off with a little cold — "

She never got to say "water," because at

that second, Chris reached for the paper towels, and he and Mal bumped heads. It was like a scene out of a Three Stooges movie.

"Gosh, I'm sorry," Chris blurted out, just as Mal started apologizing.

"Wa-a-a-a-ah!" A long wail from Claire got everyone's attention. "I want another soda," she sobbed.

"Don't worry, you'll get one right away," I said, trying to soothe her. Chris went back to filling our order while Mal and I mopped up Claire. Finally, everyone had been served, and after passing out extra napkins, I started on my ice cream.

I had only taken two bites when another disaster happened. Chris was adding extra whipped cream to Mal's strawberry sundae when he looked over his shoulder at us. His timing couldn't have been worse. The whipped-cream machine went crazy! Instead of spurting out whipped cream in neat little puffs, it blasted out clumps of cream the size of tennis balls. And it wouldn't stop.

"Oh, no!" he yelled, looking desperately around the counter for a towel. By this time, the sundae — dish and all — had turned into a giant white blob. There was whipped cream all over the counter, and a pool of whipped cream was sliding down to the floor.

"Turn it off! Pull the plug out of the wall!" someone yelled. Chris looked blankly toward the wall socket and then sprang to life. He yanked the plug just as another torrent of whipped cream buried the napkin holder.

"Wow, I don't know how that happened," he said, looking shaken. Margo and Vanessa were giggling, and Claire was laughing hysterically. Mallory looked mortified, though.

"That's okay," I said grimly, wishing we had never come into Ice-Cream Palace.

We waited while Chris made *another* sundae, and I asked him to make it a take-out. (I had already decided not to sit there a minute longer than I had to.) I was drumming my fingers on the counter when I noticed that Vanessa looked very upset.

"What's the matter?" I asked her. "That wasn't your fault."

"I know," she said in a quavery voice. I could tell that she was very close to tears.

What was going on? Why would Vanessa think she was responsible for all the problems Chris was having? I didn't have time to think about it, because people were staring at us, and I wanted to get outside as quickly as possible. The minute Mal got her sundae, I slid off the stool and we herded Claire, Margo, and Vanessa toward the door. I left my dish of Rocky Road melting on the counter, but I didn't care. For some reason, I had completely lost my taste for ice cream.

CHAPTER 6

Monday

I'm putting everyone on alert. I sat
with the Rodowsky boys today, and
Jackie Rodowsky hasn't changed a bit.
That kid should come with a survival
manual! We spent the day at the pool,
which sounds harmless but wasn't.
Everything that could go wrong, did go
wrong, thanks to you-know-who. Poor
Jackie. It's not really his fault. The
kid is a walking disaster! All BSC
members should be on their guard.
Jackie Rodowsky is hazardous to
your health....

It's times like these that make you realize how important the BSC notebook is. The "notebook" is different from the record book, in case you've forgotten. All of us are responsible for writing up every single baby-sitting job we go on. Then, once a week, we're supposed to read about the jobs in the notebook. It was Kristy's idea, and even though we complain about it, it's really very helpful. We can find out if the kids we sit for are having problems the rest of us should know about, and we can learn how to handle sticky situations (such as Kristy's problems with Jackie Rodowsky). Writing in the notebook is one of the few rules in the BSC.

Kristy's day with the Rodowsky boys started out innocently enough. (Of course, even hurricanes and flash floods start out small.) Kristy was happy to take the job, because things were getting pretty boring in Stoneybrook, and Mrs. Rodowsky offered her a whole day's work. How could she know that a day at the community pool would turn into a scene from a baby-sitting horror movie?

"Are you sure you have everything?" Mrs. Rodowsky asked. She was double-parked at the entrance to the pool, while Kristy and the boys piled out of the car. The Rodowsky boys are Archie (age four), Jackie (age seven), and Shea (age nine). All three boys have flaming red hair and plenty of freckles.

Kristy did a quick check and nodded. The kids were armed with towels, suntan lotion, and lunch money.

"We don't have Hilda," Archie complained. Hilda was a lime-green float with a head like the Loch Ness monster.

"You know we can't bring Hilda to the pool," Kristy explained. "They don't allow floats or rafts because they take up too much room."

"Floats are for babies," Shea said firmly.

"They are not!" Archie's freckles stood out on his pale skin when he was angry.

Shea shrugged and decided it wasn't worth continuing the argument. Who wanted to fight when a day at the pool stretched ahead of them?

The pool complex is much bigger than it looks from the outside. There are actually three pools — an Olympic-sized swimming pool, a wading pool, and a diving pool — plus a playground and snack bar. A first-aid station is off to one side, right next to the bathroom and showers.

"I'm starving!" Jackie announced. "Can I

buy one of those big chocolate chip cookies?"
It was ten-thirty in the morning, and they had
just walked through the gates.

"You're hungry already?" Kristy said
doubtfully.

"Yes." Jackie rubbed his stomach as if he
hadn't eaten in days.

"I guess so." Even as she said the words,
Kristy felt a little tingle of dread go through
her. Something will go wrong, she thought.
Something always goes wrong when Jackie is
involved. She settled herself on a towel,
watching as Jackie headed for the snack bar.
So far, so good. Archie and Shea were playing
in the shallow end of the pool, right next to
her, so that was no problem. But Jackie? She
just couldn't shake the nagging feeling that
something was about to happen.

A few minutes later, Jackie headed back,
carefully unwrapping his cookie. It looked
crumbly and delicious, the size of a small dinner plate.

"Look what I've got," he called happily to
his brothers.

"Hey, gimme a bite!" Archie yelled.

"No way, José." Jackie stood at the edge of
the pool, waving the cookie playfully in front
of Archie's nose. Archie made a grab for the

cookie, Jackie stepped back, and then — the cookie fell into the pool!

"Aw!" Jackie wailed.

Kristy jumped to her feet and stared at the huge cookie, which was dissolving into a zillion pieces. She felt like crying. "Quick, get one of the lifeguards," she said to Shea. She knelt at the edge of the pool, trying to scoop up the floating mess in her hands, but it was hopeless. Jackie had dropped the cookie right next to a large circulation vent (naturally!) and goo was spinning everywhere.

"Yuck! What a mess," a male voice said.

Kristy glanced up to see a lifeguard standing next to her with a net. He made a face as he tried to capture some of the floating debris.

"I'm sorry. It was an accident." Jackie's voice sounded very small, and his lower lip was trembling. Kristy put her arm around him. No wonder he was upset. Being a klutz isn't much fun.

"You're not supposed to have food in the pool area," the lifeguard said.

"I know," Jackie spoke up. "I wasn't going to eat it here. I was just unwrapping it here."

The lifeguard gave Kristy an I-don't-believe-a-word-of-this look, and walked away.

"I want to go to the diving pool," Shea announced. "I want to try a somersault."

"I want to do somersaults, too," Archie said, tugging at Kristy's hand.

"You can't do somersaults without a diving board, and you're too small to go in the diving pool," Kristy said. Things were starting to get complicated.

"I'm not too small!"

"Yes, you are. They have a height requirement. How about if I take you to the wading pool?"

"That's for babies!" Archie wailed.

Shea snickered, but Kristy stopped him with a look. "No, it's not," she said quickly. "There are a lot of big kids there. You'll see. It'll be fun. You can practice keeping your eyes open underwater."

Shea picked up his towel and headed for the diving pool while Kristy walked Archie to the wading pool. Jackie tagged along, humming to himself. It was a bright, sunny day, and for just a moment, Kristy let herself relax. Maybe things would be okay after all. Maybe there would be no new disasters.

"Aughh! Ow! Ow! OW!" Jackie was shrieking like he had stepped on a piece of glass.

"What is it?" Kristy made him sit on the concrete while she looked at his foot. "Did you step on something?"

"O-o-o-o-o-w!" (a long drawn-out wail from

59

Jackie). Kristy was puzzled. He had a small red spot on his foot, but outside of that, he looked okay.

And then she saw the dead bee.

"Look," Archie said, turning it over with his toe. "Jackie squished it."

Jackie stopped howling long enough to follow the conversation. "A bee? Oh, no! I've been bitten by a bee!" Another high-pitched shriek.

"It's all right," Kristy said soothingly. She had read up on bee stings and knew that if the wound was clean and there was no stinger inside, it was okay. Just to be on the safe side, though, she decided to march Jackie over to the first-aid station.

The nurse took charge of the situation right away. Jackie stopped crying the minute he sat on the examining table, and ten minutes later, they were back out at the pool area. Jackie was fine.

Now what? Kristy thought. It was only eleven-thirty, and she was exhausted.

"Can we eat lunch, Kristy?" Archie was pulling on her arm, and she didn't have the energy to resist. It was a little early to eat, but maybe it was safer to have everyone sitting down together. Surely nothing could happen over a plate of cheeseburgers. She rounded up Shea from the diving pool, and the two of them staked out a table, while Jackie and Archie went to the snack bar.

Then Kristy and Shea waited. And waited. Shea shifted restlessly on the wooden bench, and Kristy checked her watch. What was keeping Jackie and Archie?

"Hey, Kristy, what's going on over there?" Shea pointed to a commotion at the snack bar. It looked like someone was holding up a long line of people.

It had to be Jackie. Kristy was sure of it. "Stay here," she ordered Shea, and took off for the snack bar. She spotted Jackie at the cashier, emptying his pockets while Archie nibbled on a candy bar.

"What's going on?" she asked, trying to keep cool.

"Oh, Kristy, I'm glad you're here." Jackie gave her a winning smile. "I guess I bought too much, because I ran out of money."

She looked at his tray. It was overflowing with Mars Bars, M&M's, Devil Dogs, and Cheez Doodles. Somewhere under the mess, she saw the cheeseburgers and fries she had told him to order. "I'll say," she muttered.

Without another word, she took all the

candy and junk food off the tray and then turned to the cashier. "Please just ring up the burgers and fries."

"Kristy!" Jackie howled. She ignored him, paid the cashier, and picked up the tray. Archie gulped down the last of his candy bar — probably afraid he would have to give it back — and hurried after her.

It was much later in the afternoon when Kristy breathed a small sigh of relief. The day was almost over, and nothing else had gone wrong. Or had it? Suddenly she realized that someone was missing. Her heart hammered in her chest. There was Archie, kicking in the wading pool . . . and there was Shea, showing off in the diving pool, and Jackie . . . wait a minute . . . Jackie was missing!

Frantically, Kristy scrambled to her feet and ran a few steps to the diving pool. The crowd had thinned out since lunchtime, and it was obvious that Jackie wasn't there. She dashed to the edge of the Olympic-sized-pool.

"Jackie!" she called. A few kids stopped swimming to look at her, but she knew she was wasting her time. Don't panic, don't panic, she thought. She forced herself to slow down and take a deep breath. Racing around the pool complex was crazy. The right thing for a baby-sitter to do in a situation like this is to notify a lifeguard. Immediately.

"Don't worry, he's around somewhere," said the nearest lifeguard encouragingly. "We'll page him over the loudspeaker."

"Thanks." Kristy leaned against the lifeguard station, noticing for the first time that her legs were shaky. *Will Jackie Rodowsky please report to the lifeguard station?* The voice boomed over the address system every few seconds, with no results. Five minutes passed, then ten. Kristy felt like her heart was playing leapfrog in her chest. Where was Jackie? What would she tell Mrs. Rodowsky?

In the end, it was Shea who found him. "Here he is!" Shea said triumphantly. He was leading a puzzled-looking Jackie to the lifeguard station. "Boy, are you gonna get it!" he said happily to his brother.

"Where were you?" Kristy blurted out. Her voice was so quavery she barely recognized it. Even Jackie looked surprised.

"I was taking a shower. I wanted to get some of that chlorine out of my hair." He was looking at the lifeguard, who was going back to his post. "Were you guys actually *worried* about me?"

"We were paging you. For ten whole minutes."

"I couldn't hear you with the water running."

Kristy stared at him for a moment. There were a million things she *could* say to him, but what would be the point? Jackie was Jackie. A walking disaster!

"Look, there's Mom!" Shea yelled. "She's parked outside."

Kristy ordered everyone to pack up their beach towels and head toward the car. Four-thirty. It was hard to believe that only a few hours had passed. She stifled a yawn and helped the kids pile into the backseat. Another day with Jackie Rodowsky was finally over.

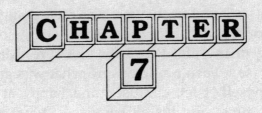

CHAPTER 7

Tuesday

Dear Dad and Sharon,

This is a super vacation! We spend practically every minute at the beach, and the Pike kids are into snorkeling. We've had just one cloudy day, but nobody minded. Stacey has a terrific tan, and I've already gone through a whole bottle of sunblock. Give Tigger a kiss for me and tell him I'll bring him back a toy!

Love You Lots,
Mary Anne

I reread my postcard and decided that it was extremely boring. It was also totally impersonal — if you knew what was *really* going on. It didn't give a clue about the exciting something in my life. Why? I'm not sure. Maybe because I wasn't exactly sure what was going on myself. I felt confused and happy at the same time, and it's all because of what happened at the beach today. . . .

The day started out in a very ordinary way. Stacey and Mal and I had just spread out our blankets on the sand, and the younger Pike kids were getting ready to hurl themselves into the water. The Pikes may be a laid-back family, but there is one hard and fast rule — no one can go in the water before nine A.M. or after five P.M. That's because those are the only hours the lifeguards are on duty.

The moment the lifeguards climbed into their seats, the kids raced down to the ocean. I put another coating of zinc oxide on my nose and pulled my straw hat down over my face. Then I put sunblock on my arms and legs, and made sure my caftan covered my knees.

While I was going through all these contortions, I noticed that Stacey and Mal were doing just the opposite. I was bundling up like an

Eskimo settling in for the winter, and they were getting ready to soak up the sun. Stacey slipped out of her cover-up and stretched out in a skimpy blue bikini. I had to admit she looked great. Her skin was the color of maple sugar, and her sun-streaked hair tumbled halfway down her back. And Mal, in a bright two-piece suit (blue bottom and striped tank top), was turning a golden brown. Her skin was catching up to her freckles.

Stacey was busily applying Sun-Lite to her hair (can you get any blonder than blonde?) when we heard the shout.

"Mary Anne! Stacey!" It was definitely a masculine voice.

"What in the world — " Stacey began.

I turned around just in time to see two teenage boys and half a dozen little kids racing toward us. The kids looked young — even younger than Margo — and I couldn't figure out who they were. Then I recognized the boy in the white cutoffs and the green-and-white-striped top. "Ohmigosh!" I cried. "It's Alex."

"And Toby," Stacey added, scrambling to her feet. "Wow," she said softly. "Doesn't he look gorgeous?"

He did. Except I couldn't really concentrate on anyone except Alex. I hadn't thought of him a lot since we'd said good-bye, but I felt a jolt when I saw him now. He looked *wonderful*.

"Mary Anne! How are you?" He was at my side then, a little out of breath. He was tall, with brown hair, and had a great smile. How could I have forgotten that smile?

"I'm fine. How are you?" I smiled back. Alex took a step toward me, as if he wanted to sweep me into a big bear hug, and then he seemed to remember we were *surrounded* by kids. It was like the Munchkin scene in *The Wizard of Oz*.

"Toby and I are working together for a whole month as mother's helpers."

"Really?" I felt incredibly happy. A whole month! I'd be able to see Alex every single day.

Alex nodded. "We found two families who were vacationing together, and they wanted two sitters for all the kids." He glanced over at Toby, who was already deep in conversation with Stacey. I noticed she had tucked the Sun-Lite bottle out of sight and was trying to dry her hair with a towel.

"Nice kids," I said, eyeing a little red-haired girl who had wrapped her arms around Alex's tanned leg.

"This is Sheila," he said, swinging her up on his shoulder. "She's two years old, and those boys are her brothers. They're twins. The other three kids are their cousins."

"And this is Mal," I said. "You remember Mallory?" Mal and Alex smiled at each other.

Claire came out of the water just then and glared at Sheila. "What's that baby doing here?" she demanded.

"Claire," I said, "that's not very nice."

Claire put her hands on her hips. "Silly-billy-goo-goo," she said to Sheila, who stuck her thumb in her mouth.

Alex laughed. "Is that some sort of code?"

"No," I said, embarrassed. "Claire just says that when she gets in one of her moods."

Alex didn't seem the least bit annoyed and knelt down so he was on eye level with Claire. "I've got a great idea," he said very seriously. "Want to hear it?" (Claire didn't say anything and looked totally unimpressed.) "Why don't we all build a sand castle?"

Claire scuffed her big toe in the sand for a full thirty seconds before answering. "That's a dumb idea," she said flatly.

"Claire!" I was shocked. Maybe Claire was feeling a little jealous of Sheila, but that was no excuse to be rude.

I started to tell her so when the other Pike kids trooped curiously out of the water, and we introduced everybody.

"Fourteen kids," Alex said, counting heads. "Definitely enough to make a monster sand castle. Anybody interested?"

"We are!" Jordan said, speaking for the triplets. "Come on, guys, let's start on the base." He turned to Sheila's twin brothers. "You can be helpers," he said generously.

We all walked down to the water's edge, and I noticed that Stacey and Toby never took their eyes off each other. Stacey seemed thrilled to see Toby again, but I reminded myself that she had acted exactly the same way around Pierre, a boy we met at a ski lodge. And there'd been Scott, the Sea City lifeguard, too. Toby was at the top of the list for the moment, but who knew if it would last?

I noticed that Sheila looked a little left out, so I took her by the hand. "I'll show you how to decorate the sand castle," I said, putting some wet sand in her hand. "Just let it dribble out slowly."

At first Sheila didn't want to touch the sand, but then she tried it and shrieked with delight. "Birthday cake," she said loudly, and Alex laughed.

"That's right. It's just like the decorations on your birthday cake."

Everything went smoothly for the next few minutes, but then Sheila's foot slipped and she accidentally kicked the castle. A portion of the wall fell away and Claire hooted.

"Stupey-silly-billy-goo-goo," she shouted, and Sheila began to cry.

"Claire!" I said sharply. "It was an accident." Then I bent down and handed Sheila a plastic shovel. "Here," I said. "I've got a very special job for you to do." She stopped crying and looked at me. "You can make a tunnel that will lead all the way to the castle." I led her to a spot a few feet away, and she started digging happily. I watched her for a moment and then stood by Alex.

"I'm really glad we ran into each other again," he said quietly.

"I'm glad, too." The understatement of the year! There were a million things I wanted to say to Alex, but I knew the beach wasn't the time or the place. Particularly with fourteen kids around. I wondered if he remembered the last night we spent together in Sea City, and if he still had the ring I gave him. (I know he wasn't wearing it, because I looked.) I even found myself wondering if he had a girlfriend back home, and if he planned on seeing me when he was in Sea City. Of course we'd see each other at the beach, but I was already hoping for more than that.

The sun was setting when Stacey and Mal and I finally rounded up all the beach towels and kids and equipment. Then Stace and I said good-bye to Alex and Toby.

"That was fun, wasn't it?" I said to Stacey as we plodded through the sand back to the house, Mal at our side, the others in front of us.

"It was fantastic," she said dreamily. "Who ever thought we'd see them again? It's just *perfect*." She paused. "Do you think they'll ask us out?"

"I don't know. I guess it depends on whether they can get any time off."

Mal looked aghast, and I had a feeling she was thinking of Logan. I shook off pangs of guilt.

Stacey stretched out her arms to inspect her tan. "From the look on Toby's face, he'll *make* the time."

I could feel the heat rising in my cheeks. I blush *very* easily, as any of my friends will tell you. "I'm not so sure about Alex."

"Ha! Believe me, I am. He was staring at you so hard, I thought his eyes were going to fall out of his head. If I were Logan, I'd be worried right about now."

"Logan has nothing to worry about," I said stiffly. (Mal raised her eyebrows.)

Stacey considered what I'd said and then giggled. "Do you mean, what he doesn't know won't hurt him?"

I turned to look at her. "No, I mean Logan doesn't have to worry because I will *always* be true to him. He's my boyfriend and always will be."

I raised my voice without meaning to, because I was feeling so confused. It was amazing, but I hadn't even *thought* of Logan until now. I meant what I said about Logan being my boyfriend. But could a visit from Alex change all that? I didn't have an answer. Suddenly nothing was making any sense at all.

CHAPTER 8

Friday

Dear Claudia,

You're not going to
believe this, but Alex
and Toby are back in
Sea City! They're working
as mother's helpers, and
we ran into them on
the beach. This is
shaping up to be a very
interesting vacation,
and I have no idea
what will happen next.
Suddenly there are so
many boys around here,
we're practically tripping
over them. Even Vanessa

met a boy she likes at
Ice-Cream Palace.
Furthermore, Stacey and I
had sort of a fight....
                    Love,
                Mary Anne

There was a big mix-up Friday night. It wasn't Stacey's fault, but it wasn't my fault, either. (And I'm the one who got stuck.) This is the way it happened. Mr. and Mrs. Pike said that Stacey and I could have one evening off each week, but they asked us to take the evenings *separately*. I could see their point. That way they could go out every evening if they wanted to, knowing that Mal and either Stacey or I would baby-sit. Stacey and I were a little disappointed with the arrangement because we liked evenings off together, but we didn't say anything. We didn't even talk about it, which was a shame, because we should have straightened out our nights off in the beginning.

The first inkling I had that something was wrong was when I saw Stacey drag out the iron. It was six-thirty on Friday evening, and we had just cleaned up the kitchen after an early supper. Stacey *hates* to iron, and I was amazed to see her spread a white cotton sundress over the ironing board in the corner of the kitchen.

"You're ironing?" I said incredulously.

Stacey touched her finger to her nose like you do in charades when someone guesses the right word.

I felt a little silly. It was pretty obvious that she was ironing, the question was . . . why? "I meant, why are you doing that now?"

Stacey looked up, her blue eyes very bright against her tanned face. "Well, I can't go out on a date with a wrinkled dress, can I?"

"A date?"

"With Toby." She bent over the sundress, humming a little song. She suddenly looked a little pale, even under her suntan, and I wondered if she felt okay. Stacey's diabetes is under control, but she has to watch her diet and medication. "We're going to the arcade tonight. You don't think this is too dressy, do you?" she asked worriedly. She didn't wait for me to answer, which is just as well, because I was standing there with my mouth hanging open. "I want to wear white because it will show off my tan."

"You're going to the arcade?" I blurted out. "Tonight?"

"It will certainly bring back memories," she

said with a sigh. I knew exactly what she meant. The last time she went to the arcade, she and Toby had had what you would call a very romantic evening. He won a stuffed teddy bear for her, which she immediately named "Toby-Bear." But the really *big* news was that they went through the Tunnel of Luv, where Toby gave Stacey her first kiss.

"I remember the last time we went to the arcade," she began. "It was such an *incredible* evening — "

I could tell Stacey was revving up for a lot of mushy memories, but I had something more important on my mind. If Stacey was going out with Toby that night, I had to say something — fast!

"Um, Stacey," I said, "I'm afraid there's a problem."

"A problem?" She blinked and put the iron on its end. At last I had her full attention.

"I'm going out tonight. With Alex."

"What?!" She managed to put a lot of emotion into that one word, and it wasn't surprise. It was outrage.

"That's right. Alex. Tonight. At eight." I didn't want to mention that we were planning on going to the arcade. There was no point in making her feel worse than she already did.

I thought she'd head straight for the phone to cancel with Toby, but she surprised me. She went right back to ironing!

"Stacey, did you hear me?"

"Of course," she said smoothly. "You'll just have to cancel with Alex. What a shame." She was very matter-of-fact about it.

Now it was my turn to be outraged. "Why should *I* cancel?" I demanded. "You had no right to make a date without asking me."

Stacey's eyes widened. "I don't need your permission to go out with Toby."

"You mean you just took it for granted that I'd stay home with Mal and the kids?"

"Well, one of us has to be here," she said reasonably. "And anyway, all you have to do is tell Alex you'll see him tomorrow night."

She flounced up to our room to get changed and left me fuming in the kitchen. I couldn't believe that Stacey was being so selfish.

I was still thinking about our fight as Mal and I helped the kids get ready for bed that night. I went into Vanessa's room to close the window, while Mal helped Claire and Margo.

"Mary Anne," she said, "can you stay and talk to me for a minute?"

"Sure." I sat down on the edge of the bed. "What's up?"

"I've been doing some writing," she said.

She reached under the bed and pulled out a notepad and a ballpoint pen.

"Poems?" I asked.

"Well," she said, "yes. But different from the usual ones. I'm writing some poems for Chris. You know, the boy at Ice-Cream Palace." I must have looked surprised because she added, "I have this big crush on him. I think he's adorable, don't you?"

"Well, yes. He's really cute."

"Here, read them and tell me what you think." She shoved the notebook at me and I quickly scanned a page. It was obvious that Vanessa was *crazy* over Chris. How could this have happened? I wondered. She didn't even know him!

An accident brought us together,
And I know we will never part.
Please say you'll love me forever,
You've totally stolen my heart.

"Very nice." I handed her the notebook. What else could I say?

"I wrote eight all together. I just hope he likes them." She snuggled down under the covers.

"You're going to show Chris the poems?" A little warning bell went off in my head. Somehow I knew this wasn't such a great idea.

"Of course not," she said with a laugh. "I want to be his secret admirer. It wouldn't be much of a secret if he knew who wrote them, would it?"

"I guess not." I paused. "What exactly are you going to do with them?"

"I thought I'd leave them on the counter at Ice-Cream Palace, where he'll be sure to find them." She yawned and started to close her eyes. "He'll be so surprised," she said, her voice already trailing off.

"I'm sure he will be," I replied. I got up quietly and tucked the quilt around her. First Alex and Toby (not to mention Logan and Pierre) and now this. Things were getting too complicated and the reason was obvious. There were just too many boys!

CHAPTER 9

Saturday

Last night I had a "surprise" baby-sitting job. It was all my father's idea. His girlfriend Carol showed up with an eight-month-old boy and a three-year-old girl. They were very cute, but I wasn't thrilled when Dad asked me to sit for them so he and Carol could go to a play. How could I refuse, though? It's lucky Jeff was home, because he turned out to be a great baby-sitter. By the way, if any of you BSC members have advice on what to do for colicky babies, I hope you'll write it in the notebook....

Dawn had almost forgotten how relaxing it was in California. She loved everything about the place. The sunny climate, the sparkling ocean, the big roomy house with the tile floors and slanted skylights. Life was so . . . carefree, she decided, stretching out on a chaise lounge on the redwood deck. Her father had a great housekeeper, Mrs. Bruen, who looked after everything and cooked all of Dawn's favorite foods. And Dawn enjoyed seeing her younger brother, Jeff, again. He was *much* happier since he had left Stoneybrook to live in California with his father.

Life was almost perfect, she decided, munching on an avocado salad that Mrs. Bruen had prepared for lunch. There was only one nagging problem that wouldn't go away, and her name was Carol. Carol was her father's girlfriend, and she rubbed Dawn the wrong way. Dawn couldn't say exactly why she didn't like Carol, but there was something about her that was very annoying. For one thing, she was always *there*. She spent so much time at the house, you'd think she was part of the family. And Dawn didn't like it one bit.

The doorbell rang later that afternoon, just as Dawn was heading inside to take a shower.

She had spent the whole day soaking up the rays in her bikini, and she was covered in baby oil.

"Sunshine, get the door, will you?" Dawn's father called from the kitchen. Sunshine was his nickname for her.

Dawn threw open the front door and felt like someone had doused her with cold water. Her good mood vanished as she tied her cover-up around her.

"Hi there!" Carol said brightly. "Look what I brought!" She was holding a baby in her arms, and a solemn-looking little girl clung to her leg.

Dawn's father hurried into the foyer.

"Well, well, what do we have here?" Dawn knew he was surprised but was trying hard not to show it.

"Aren't they adorable?" Carol said in a gushy voice that Dawn hated. "This is Gregory. He's only eight months old. And this is his sister, Julie." She pulled Julie out from the folds of her sundress. "Julie's three."

"But who *are* they?" Dawn said pointedly. She knew they weren't Carol's children.

"That's a long story," Carol said as they made their way into the living room. She tossed a diaper bag on the floor and settled

Gregory on her lap. "One of my old friends from college is visiting California with her husband. They couldn't get a sitter, so I told her I'd watch her kids tonight so they can go out."

"That was very nice of you," Mr. Schafer said slowly, "but it complicates things a little."

"What things?"

Mr. Schafer sat down next to her. "Do you remember that musical you wanted to see at the Playhouse?"

"The one that's sold out?"

"Well, it's not completely sold out." Mr. Schafer reached into his pocket and pulled out two tickets. "One of my clients got me two of the best seats in the house for tonight."

"Oh, no!" Carol wailed. "Why didn't you tell me?"

"I wanted it to be a surprise."

Dawn stood watching this scene, wondering how she could make a polite escape. She was sorry if her father was disappointed, but it didn't affect her, did it?

A moment later, she realized it did.

"Say, I've got an idea," her father said suddenly. He turned around and stared at Dawn as if he were seeing her for the first time. "What are you and Jeff doing tonight?"

Dawn licked her lips nervously. She knew

what was coming. "We're, uh . . . going to rent a video, I think."

"Perfect!" Mr. Schafer clapped his hands. "You and the kids can all watch the video together."

Dawn looked at him. The idea of a little baby watching a video was so ridiculous she didn't know what to say. "You mean you want me to baby-sit the kids?" she said tightly.

"Well, you're not doing anything anyway," Mr. Schafer said, looking very pleased.

"Oh, could you?" Carol said, jumping to her feet. "That would be wonderful!"

"And I'll pay you," Mr. Schafer said.

"Well . . ."

"Then it's all settled." Mr. Schafer reached for Carol's hand. "Wait till you see what we're cooking on the grill tonight. . . ."

"This is *not* my idea of a great evening," Jeff said a few hours later. He was trying to watch an Indiana Jones movie, but Gregory was crying. He was making more noise than the soundtrack. "What do you think is wrong with him, anyway?"

"Carol said he has colic," Dawn replied. She really felt sorry for Gregory, because she knew he was in pain. His legs were doubled up and he seemed to howl no matter what she did. She had tried *everything*, rocking him, singing to him, but he cried louder than ever. The only thing that really worked was pacing up and down the floor with him.

It was a baby-sitter's nightmare, and she knew she wasn't being fair to Julie, who was wandering around the living room with nothing to do.

"Oh, let's watch this tomorrow," Jeff said, rewinding the video. He looked at Julie, who was staring blankly out the window. "Hey, Julie," he said suddenly. "How about a game?"

"We don't have any kiddie games," Dawn reminded him. Naturally Carol hadn't brought any toys for the kids.

"We have a deck of cards," Jeff answered.

"She's too young for cards."

"Cards," Julie repeated, walking over to him.

"We're not going to play cards, we're going to build a *house* of cards," Jeff told Dawn.

For the next hour, Julie was fascinated as Jeff showed her how to place the cards on top of each other to make a house. "Gently, gently," he warned, as she laid the top card in place. "If you even breathe on it, it will all fall down." When they finished playing with the cards, Jeff made up a story about a cowardly dragon who wanted to be friends with a lion, and Julie giggled when he made funny faces. Then he showed her how to make shadow puppets on the white stucco walls, and invented animal voices to go with the shapes. Finally, a happy, tired Julie fell asleep on the rug.

Dawn was amazed. "You were great," she whispered. "I had no idea you were so good with kids."

"What can I say?" Jeff laughed. He put a blanket over Julie and looked at Gregory. "He's asleep, too."

"Can you believe it?" Dawn said wearily. "Let's try carrying them and putting them both in my bed."

"So far, so good," Jeff said a few minutes later when they'd returned to the living room. He looked up at the ceiling, as if he expected to hear crying any minute.

"What do you think is going to happen with Dad and Carol?" Dawn said. She curled up on the sofa, hugging a throw pillow to her chest.

Jeff shrugged. He minded Carol just as much as Dawn did, but he felt a little uncomfortable talking about her. "He likes her, that's all."

"Are you sure it's not serious? She's over here all the time."

"That doesn't mean anything. Dad's not going to go off the deep end and marry her or anything like that."

"How can you be so sure?"

Jeff shrugged. "I just know he's not. You worry too much."

Dawn was about to say something else, but Jeff reached for the remote control. In a moment, Harrison Ford's face filled the screen, and Dawn tried to put all her fears behind her.

"You did a great job tonight," Mr. Schafer said a couple of hours later. He handed Dawn a wad of bills, and Dawn stifled a yawn. This had been one of the toughest baby-sitting jobs she had ever had.

"Thanks," she mumbled, heading for her door. She was halfway to the doorway when she stopped and walked back to the kitchen. Jeff was at the counter, making himself an enormous sandwich of Swiss cheese and sprouts. "Here," she said, offering him half of the money. "This is for you."

"That's okay." He grinned and waved his hand.

"No way," she said, tucking the bills into his shirt pocket. "You earned every penny of it." As she headed for bed, a funny thought crossed her mind: Maybe someday Jeff would be a baby-sitter, too!

CHAPTER 10

Saturday

Dear Logan,

More of the same. Perfect weather, great swimming, and the kids are still getting along with each other. What could be better? Wish you were here.

Love,
Mary Anne

Talk about a guilty conscience! I had a terrible time trying to figure out what to say to Logan, because I was afraid he would read between the lines. I finally decided that the less said, the better. You'll notice I didn't mention Alex. How could I? I felt silly leaving him out, but I didn't dare tell Logan what was really going on. . . .

I was so excited Saturday afternoon, I was practically floating. This is what happened. When I called Alex to explain that I wouldn't be able to see him Friday night (all because of Stacey), he immediately asked me out for Saturday. We were going to have dinner at a seafood place, and I spent half an hour trying on every single outfit I had brought with me. Nothing looked right. I had plenty of casual clothes, but we were going to a "real" restaurant (unlike Burger Garden), and I wanted to be dressed up.

I had just decided to ask Stacey if I could borrow her red sundress when she walked into the bedroom, drying her hair. You can imagine how surprised I was when she pulled the red sundress out of the closet and tossed it on the bed!

"Wow, you must have read my mind," I told her.

"Why's that?" She ran her fingers through her damp hair.

"I was just going to ask you if I could borrow that."

Stacey shrugged and peeled off her T-shirt. "Normally I'd say yes, but I need it myself tonight."

"Oh, sure," I said quickly. "I understand." I really hate borrowing things, and I didn't want to put her on the spot. Then it hit me! "Wait a minute," I said, taking a step toward her. "Why do *you* need a dress for tonight?"

Stacey plunked herself down at the dressing table and started fumbling with bottles of nail polish. "I'm wearing it out to dinner." She was absolutely calm. I couldn't believe it.

"You're going to dinner? On a *date?*" I squawked.

She hesitated, just for a second. "Um, yes, that's right."

"Stacey McGill, you are unbelievable!" I sat down on the bed and just stared at her. She refused to look at me and starting painting her long fingernails with a base coat. "You went out last night, remember?" Stacey opened her mouth to say something, but I didn't give her a chance. "Here's a news flash for you. *I* am going out tonight." I paused. "*You* are staying home with the kids. That was our arrangement."

I picked up my towel and headed for the shower, my face flaming. Stacey caught up with me in the hall, and I was glad to see she had ruined her nails by jumping up so fast.

"Look, Mary Anne," she said in a wheedling tone, "I didn't mean to upset you. It's just that Toby and I had such a *fantastic* time last night that I thought you wouldn't mind if I went out with him again."

"You thought I wouldn't mind?" I said coolly. My heart was pounding in my chest, but I stood my ground.

"You can take off two nights *next* week," she said. You'd think she was doing me a big favor. "That would be fair, wouldn't it?"

"No, Stacey. It would *not* be fair. I'm going out tonight, and if you'll excuse me, I need to get ready." I brushed by her and headed for the shower without another word.

"This is very nice," I said later that evening. Alex and I were sitting in a back booth at the restaurant, looking over the menu. The menu was enormous — about the size of a cookie sheet — and I had no idea what to order. The truth is, I felt a little nervous sitting across from Alex. Going to the boardwalk was one thing, but being all dressed up in a restaurant made everything seem different somehow. Like we were on a real date. The more I tried to figure it out, the more confused I got. This was what I wanted, wasn't it? A "real" date with Alex? But what about Logan?

Alex interrupted my thoughts. "Earth to Mary Anne," he said playfully. The waitress was standing over us, order pad in hand. Ready or not, I *had* to order something!

"Um, I guess I'll have the crab cakes," I said, not really caring. "With fries and iced tea."

The minute the waitress left, we just stared at each other. In dead silence. What in the world were we going to talk about?

"Wow, we got here at a good time," I said at last.

Alex looked blank. "A good time?"

"It's not crowded now. You know, it's not too early and it's not too late." I stammered a little, feeling nervous.

Even Alex couldn't think of anything to say to *that* dumb remark, and he gazed at a point somewhere over my head. I was very tempted to turn around, but I knew that there was nothing behind me except a giant flounder that was mounted on the wall.

Another long pause. "They sure have a lot of fish on the menu," I said, thinking of the flounder. I could have bitten my tongue the minute the words were out. Of course they had a lot of fish on the menu. What did I expect at a seafood restaurant — pizza?

Alex nodded politely, but I knew he must think I was incredibly boring. Why couldn't I think of anything interesting to talk about like other girls could? I made a mental note to ask Stacey what *she* talked about on dates, and then I remembered that she was probably still mad at me. She was baby-sitting the Pike kids with Mallory, instead of having dinner with a date in a restaurant — and for just a moment, I envied them!

I think we would have gone on this way *forever*, except that something really funny happened, and we both cracked up. When the waitress served Alex his lobster, she put a *bib* on him! It was just like the kind babies wear, except it was adult-sized and had a giant lobster printed on it. Alex didn't look surprised (I guess he had ordered lobster before and knew what to expect), but I was so amazed I burst out laughing! I didn't even try to keep a straight face, and when Alex saw me laughing, *he* started laughing, and everything was okay.

After the bib incident, we had a million things to say to each other, and we talked nonstop for the rest of the meal.

Later, we hit the boardwalk, where Alex played a ringtoss game, trying to win a stuffed animal for me. After about twenty minutes (and a dozen quarters) he finally *did* win, and I picked out a big purple hippopotamus as my prize.

"You're sure you don't want a panda?" he said, eyeing the hippo. "Or maybe one of the chimpanzees?"

"Nope." I clutched my prize. "A purple hippo is just the thing."

I don't know what to tell you about the rest of the evening, except that it was wonderful. We spent another hour or so wandering up and down the midway and finally took a ride on the Ferris wheel. Alex grumbled because I had the purple hippo wedged on the seat between us, but I knew he was just kidding.

It was a beautiful starry night, and we pointed out the constellations to each other as we walked back to the Pikes'. (He picked out the Seven Sisters, but I found the Little Dipper.) Neither one of us wanted the evening to end, and Alex made a joke as I headed up the porch steps.

"Oh, Mary Anne," he said seriously. "Can I ask you a favor?"

I turned around, surprised. "Sure, what is it?"

He grinned. "The next time we go out, would you mind leaving your friend at home?"

I hugged the hippo tightly to my chest and waved good night. When I got upstairs to my bedroom, I sat on the window seat and stared out at the ocean for a long time. *The next time we go out . . .* This was what I wanted, wasn't it? Alex was so funny and sweet — of course I wanted to see him again! Then why did I feel so guilty? *Because you said you would always be true to Logan*, a little voice nagged me.

I heard Stacey moving around downstairs in the kitchen, and I quickly slipped into my nightgown and got into bed. I didn't feel like talking to anyone. It had been a wonderful, exciting, confusing evening, and there was so much to think about. . . .

CHAPTER 11

Wednesday

Dear Jessi,
Everything here has gotten very complicated, and it's all because of a boy, a bunch of love poems, and a case of mistaken identity. It sounds just like something out of Shakespeare, but I swear that it's true. I have no idea how everything will turn out, but I have the feeling that it will get worse before it gets better. I will keep you posted! Love to everyone in Stoneybrook,

MaryAnne

"**Y**ou're sure you want to go into town to-day?" It was nine-thirty in the morning, and Stacey and I had just finished cleaning up the breakfast dishes.

"Of course we're sure!" Vanessa said impatiently. "We *love* Sea City, don't we, Margo?"

Margo nodded, eager to escape a boring game of Candy Land with Claire.

"So can we? Can we *please?*" Vanessa chanted, practically jumping up and down in excitement.

"Go ahead," Stacey said, seeing my hesitation. "I'll take the boys to the beach as soon as they get changed."

"I'll go with you," added Mal. "My tan's not nearly good enough yet."

"Yippee!" Vanessa hooted, throwing her sun visor in the air.

Looking back, I'm surprised I didn't catch on to the *real* reason that Vanessa was so eager to go into town. (If you've already guessed that it was because of a certain boy named Chris, you're right.)

It was almost eleven by the time the four of us — Claire, Margo, Vanessa, and myself — stepped onto the boardwalk. It was a cool day, and Sea City was crowded with tourists.

"Can we look at souvenirs?" Margo asked.

"I brought my money with me."

We made our first stop at a little shop that sold hundreds of souvenirs made of seashells. There were jewelry boxes decorated with pearly pink shells that looked like fans, and mirrors ringed with tiny white shells no bigger than a dime. There was a music box shaped like a clam shell, and dozens of shell key rings. Everything seemed a little expensive for Margo, so I tried to persuade her to buy a plain conch shell.

"But it doesn't say Sea City on it," she said.

"But it's pretty, and every time you look at it, you'll think of the ocean," I pointed out.

Margo looked unconvinced, and Vanessa was getting impatient with her. "Don't make such a big deal out of it, Margo. Do you want to buy a seashell or not?"

"But that's just a plain old shell. I can find one of those on the beach."

"But you haven't found one yet," Vanessa said reasonably. "How about this?" She picked up a beautiful white sand dollar and handed it to Margo. Someone had drilled a hole in the top and tied a strand of ribbon through it.

"Ooh, that's pretty," Margo said. "What is it?"

"It's a Christmas tree ornament," I told her.

"You can hang it on the tree every year, and when it's snowing in Stoneybrook, you can dream about Sea City."

"I love it!" Margo cried. She had exactly enough money to pay for it, and Vanessa took her to the cashier while I wandered around the store for a few more minutes. I saw a black T-shirt that I knew Dawn would love. "Sea City" was scrawled across it in bright pink letters that looked like they were written in lipstick. It was exactly right for Dawn — but not for me — and I finally bought two coffee mugs, one for my father and one for Sharon. They looked handmade and said SEA CITY in *very* small letters at the bottom. I even found a toy for Tigger.

Our next stop was Trampoline Land, which is one of Margo's favorite spots in town. She immediately pulled Claire onto a giant trampoline with her, while Vanessa and I watched from the sidelines. I always feel a little dizzy when I watch people jump up and down on a trampoline, and I can't understand why Margo likes it so much. What is even stranger is that Margo gets motion sickness just from riding in a car, but trampolines don't seem to bother her.

Except this time.

Margo had been jumping like a human pogo

stick for almost twenty minutes when I noticed that she looked a little pale. "She looks kind of . . . white, doesn't she?" I said to no one in particular.

Vanessa gasped. "White — she looks green!" She grabbed my arm. "Mary Anne, we have to do something fast. She's going to be sick!"

"Oh, no," I moaned. I looked at Margo's head bobbing up and down and I realized that Vanessa was right. Margo's eyes were glassy, and her skin was suddenly flushed. She was *definitely* sick, and in a moment or two, everyone would know about it. "But what can we do? Why doesn't she stop?"

Vanessa shook her head. "She can't stop. She's probably trying to work her way over to the edge right now, but all those other kids are in the way. You can't just walk off a trampoline, you know."

Vanessa was absolutely right. When you're on a trampoline, you bounce up and down, even if you don't want to. Sometimes parents go on the trampoline to get their kids, and they bob up and down just like everybody else.

"I'm going in after her," I said, coming to a decision. I felt pretty silly bouncing like a kangaroo toward Margo, but after all, I was the baby-sitter. I knew I had to get to her. "Hang on, Margo," I said when I finally caught up with her. I grabbed her arm to guide her off the trampoline, and she stood on the sidelines for a few moments, swaying back and forth. Claire stood next to us.

"As soon as she feels better, we'll leave," I said to Vanessa and Claire.

"Good," Vanessa spoke up. "I want to go to Ice-Cream Palace."

I was shocked. "Vanessa, give Margo a few minutes to recover. She nearly got sick."

Vanessa rolled her eyes. "Ice cream settles your stomach," she said. No one believed her, and we headed for Fred's Putt-Putt Course to watch the miniature golf.

"*Now* can we go to Ice-Cream Palace?" Vanessa asked half an hour later. I've never known Vanessa to be so incredibly whiny.

"I guess so," I said. "Margo seems to be feeling better, and — " I never got a chance to finish the sentence because Vanessa raced ahead of me. What was the big deal about going to Ice-Cream Palace? (I should have known!)

"There he is," Vanessa said happily when we caught up with her at the Palace. She was speaking very quietly so only I could hear her. She nodded toward the counter and I saw that Chris was on duty. "I've left him three poems," she said proudly.

"You did what?"

"I managed to come here three times since last Friday," she whispered. "And I left him a note on the counter each time."

"I didn't think you were really going to do that." I felt awful and wished I had spent more time trying to talk Vanessa out of it.

"I told you I was," she said flatly. "That's the only way for him to know how I feel about him." She smiled. "And pretty soon, I'll know how he feels about me."

Chris caught sight of us then, and to my surprise, he started a conversation with Vanessa. Could he really be interested in her? I wondered. He seemed *very* curious about where we lived, and how long we were staying in Sea City. In between all the questions, he managed to make four hot fudge sundaes for us, and this time, there weren't any accidents. I noticed that his boss was keeping an eye on him, so I think he was being extra careful.

Vanessa dawdled over her sundae *forever*, probably hoping to hear more from Chris, but finally it was time to leave. We were almost out the door when Chris came dashing over, wiping his hands on his apron.

"Hey, Vanessa?" He kept his voice so low, I had to strain to hear him.

"Yes?"

"Do me a favor, will you?"

"Sure!"

"Tell Mallory I'll be able to go out with her Saturday night."

Vanessa was speechless, and so was I. He was going out with Mallory on Saturday night? How in the world had this happened?

He didn't even *know* Mallory. And Mallory probably didn't like him, so why did he think — Then it hit me. The poems! Somehow Chris had misunderstood the poems. He must have thought they were from Mallory. I struggled to remember the one that I read. Something about "an accident brought us together." Of course! He remembered bumping heads with Mallory, so naturally he thought of her when he read that line. What a mess!

In a crazy way, it made sense. After all, Chris is twelve, and Mal is eleven. Vanessa is only nine, and at that age there is a big difference. Chris probably thinks of Vanessa as a baby — but of Mal as a cute girl.

I waited until we were on the boardwalk before whispering to Vanessa, "What are you going to do?"

Vanessa shook her head, her eyes very

bright. "I don't know," she said sadly. "How could I have been so stupid?"

Claire interrupted us then, and we didn't get a chance to continue the conversation. Things were really busy at the Pikes' when we got back, and when I finally had a free moment, Mrs. Pike said Vanessa was taking a nap.

A nap at four-thirty in the afternoon? I tiptoed upstairs and stood for a minute outside her closed door. There was no sound coming from inside, and after a moment I went back downstairs. I was very worried about Vanessa.

CHAPTER 12

Thursday

It started out as the world's easiest baby-sitting job and turned into a manhunt. Or I should say a hamster hunt! I was sitting for Becca and Squirt, and it was so hot we decided to stay indoors with the air-conditioning. Becca and Charlotte Johanssen were playing Candy Store, Squirt was toddling around the house as usual, and I was stretched out with a book. And then it happened! Becca and Charlotte discovered that

Frodo, the Pikes' hamster, was missing from his cage. I told myself not to panic and tried to think of all the places a hamster might hide. Losing a pet has got to be one of the worst things that could happen to a baby-sitter, and I just hope it doesn't happen to anyone else....

It was one of those days when you are sure that nothing interesting will ever happen, and then, pow! Something zaps you right out of the blue. Jessi Ramsey was sitting for Becca and Squirt while her mother was at a job interview and her father was at work. She was happy when Charlotte Johanssen came to the door and asked if she could play with Becca. Charlotte is an only child and a favorite with the BSC members, especially Stacey. She's one of those good-natured kids, smart with a serious, adult side to her. She and Becca get along very well together, and both have good imaginations.

"Want to play Chutes and Ladders?" Becca asked. "Or Spill and Spell?"

"I don't really feel like a board game, do you?" Charlotte said, curling up on the window seat. "Let's act out something."

"Okay!" Becca said eagerly. Becca loves to pretend and can imitate any animal you can name. For instance, when she's a cat, she meows and rubs her head against your leg until you reach down and pet her. "Let's play Candy Store," she suggested.

Candy Store is a game that can go on *forever* because Becca and Charlotte each take turns being the store owner and the customer — and they both like candy.

"What kind of licorice twists do you have?" Jessi heard Becca ask. Charlotte was kneeling behind the coffee table, pretending it was a candy counter.

"We have some new cherry-flavored twists," Charlotte said, pointing to a blank spot on the coffee table. "They're absolutely delicious. And of course we have our regular black licorice ropes. Would you like to try one? We give free samples."

"I can't make up my mind," Becca said, rubbing her chin. "I came in here because I wanted something really different."

"Something *really* different? Well, you've

come to the right place." Charlotte reached down under the coffee table and pretended to lift out a tray of goodies. "These just came in today."

"What are they?"

"Licorice root-beer barrels! See, they're shaped like little barrels but they taste like licorice."

"Wow, that is different."

Charlotte looked pleased. "We're the only store in Stoneybrook that carries them. . . ."

Jessi let snatches of the girls' conversation drift in and out of her head while she kept an eye on Squirt and read a horse story. Squirt is a pretty steady walker and the Ramseys' house is completely baby-proofed, so she didn't worry when he wandered out to the kitchen and didn't come back for a few minutes.

She kept one of his favorite children's programs on TV, in case he decided to come back to the den and settle down with her. She liked to watch the show herself, because it had very good actors and some interesting skits. She idly watched as two little boys became friends, and then went back to her reading when they talked about the letter S.

Soon a jingle caught her attention, and she looked up to watch a matching game. The neighborhood kids were asked to figure out which things were alike and which things were different. It was fun, and there was a lot of giggling as the kids decided that an egg-beater didn't belong with a dog and a cat and a pig.

"Why not?" asked the host.

"Because it's different," the kids shouted.

"And what *should* go with the dog and cat and pig?"

"The goat!"

"Why?"

"Because those things are the *same*. They're all animals."

"You're absolutely right!"

Jessi heard someone clapping enthusiastically behind her and turned to see that Squirt was sitting on the floor. "Hey, Squirt, did you like that?"

Squirt didn't answer. He wandered back to the kitchen then, and Jessi returned to her book. Twenty minutes later, disaster struck. Becca and Charlotte came flying into the den.

"Jessi!" Becca cried. "Frodo's missing!"

Jessi jumped to her feet. "Frodo? That's impossible. I fed him this morning and he was curled up in his cage."

"Not anymore," Charlotte piped up.

Jessi ran out to the kitchen and saw the

111

empty cage. "Oh, no!" she wailed. She had been watching Frodo for the Pikes, and she'd been *very* careful with him. She knew a lot about hamsters because of Misty, and she knew that you have to keep them in their cages unless you're changing their litter or playing with them. You can't just let them run around the house, or they're bound to get lost.

"What should we do?" Becca asked.

"Start searching!" Jessi said. "Let's split up. We'll have to cover the whole house. He could be anywhere."

"But where should we start?" Charlotte looked around the kitchen.

Jessi thought for a moment. "I'm pretty sure he's hiding somewhere in the house." (She wouldn't even let herself *think* that he might be outside.) "We'll have to look under all the tables and chairs. Hamsters like to hide, so you'll have to check any place that he could fit under. And don't forget the closets."

Fifteen minutes later, Becca yelled down the stairs, "Jessi! Come up to my room. I found him!"

"Thank goodness. Where was he?" Jessi rushed upstairs to find Charlotte and Becca both kneeling down in front of Misty's cage. She was amazed to see *two* furry bodies munching on hamster pellets. "He's in Misty's cage!"

"Yeah, but how did he get there?" Becca reached in to pet him.

Jessi shook her head. She was baffled. "I have no idea. He certainly didn't open the cage door himself."

Becca and Charlotte laughed at the idea.

"Now what?" Charlotte asked.

Jessi opened the cage and carefully lifted out a wriggling Frodo. "He's going right back where he belongs," she said firmly. "Back to his own cage in the kitchen."

On the way downstairs she started thinking over what had just happened. There was only one explanation: Becca. Maybe Becca had thought it would be funny to put Frodo in with Misty, or maybe she thought Frodo was lonely. She decided it was time to speak up. "Becca," she said, "I know you didn't mean to do anything wrong, but it wasn't a good idea to put Frodo in with Misty — "

"But I didn't!" Becca protested. "I didn't go anywhere near him."

"Now, Becca," she said gently, "Frodo didn't *let* himself in the cage."

"But I didn't do it!" Becca repeated. "I would never do something like that. Maybe they wouldn't like each other, or maybe Frodo would eat Misty's food. You know I would never do anything that might hurt Misty."

Jessi knew that this was true. Then what had really happened?

A few minutes later, she was carefully putting Frodo back in his own cage when Squirt started yelling. "No, no! Same! Same!"

Jessi looked up. "What's the matter, Squirt?" She shut the cage door and went to the sink to wash her hands.

Squirt rushed to the cage and tried to open it. "Open!" he demanded.

Jessi knelt down so she was at eye level with him. "Frodo belongs in his own cage," she said, but Squirt went right on yelling.

"Same, same!"

Finally Jessi got it. Squirt had put the two hamsters in the same cage because they were the same! He'd really been paying attention to the TV show.

"Wow," she said softly. Squirt was obviously a genius. She could hardly wait to tell her parents that her baby brother was *much* smarter than anyone had guessed.

CHAPTER 13

Friday

Dear Kristy,
 I never thought I'd
say this, but Stacey is
driving me crazy! She's
going through a bad
time, and she's taking
it out on me. In case
you're wondering, it's all
because of a boy. Boys
really complicate things,
don't they? I can't
believe that we're leaving
Sea City tomorrow. It's
been fun, but in some
ways I can hardly wait
to be back in Stoneybrook.

By the time you get this post card, you'll probably know the whole story.
Love,
MaryAnne

I didn't want to say too much in the postcard, but Stacey and I have not been getting along very well. It's all because Toby *dumped* her on Thursday night. I didn't find out about it until Friday morning after breakfast.

Stacey came charging out of the bathroom, her face like a thundercloud. "You used my towel — again!" she yelled.

"I did *not* use your towel," I said quietly. I hate it when people get mad at me, but I wasn't going to confess to something I didn't do. I've found that the best thing to do when Stacey gets in one of her moods is to ignore her, and that's just what I did.

"How can you stand there and deny it?" she demanded. She walked right up to me, so close our noses were practically touching.

"Stacey," I said, trying to keep my cool, "*my* towel has blue flowers with yellow centers. *Your* towel has yellow flowers with blue centers."

116

She frowned. "Yellow flowers with — "

"That's right." I turned away and started folding my shorts and T-shirts into a pile. I knew it would be hectic tomorrow when we had to close up the house.

"Humph," she snorted. "Well, maybe you're right about the towel," she admitted. She stood staring at me, and I could practically see the wheels turning. She was *looking* for something to get mad about. "I can't believe you're doing this *now*," she said, pointing to the stack of clothes.

"I like to be organized," I said, sighing, "and things will be really busy in the morning."

"You're *always* organized," she said coolly. "I would find it *very* boring to live that way."

"Uh-huh." I looked at Stacey's cosmetics strewn over the dresser. Not much danger of that, I thought.

She ran her finger lightly along the edge of my T-shirts. "You're so neat, I'm surprised you don't iron your underwear." She paused. "Or maybe you do when we're all asleep." She flounced out of the room before I could think up an answer to that one.

I didn't find out about Toby until that evening. Stacey had calmed down a little after dinner, and she and Mal and I were sitting on the porch swing. It was dusk, my favorite time of day, and a salty breeze was blowing off the ocean.

"I guess tonight is the time for good-byes," I said quietly.

"Toby already said good-bye. Last night," she sniffled. She buried her face in her hands, just for a minute.

"Stacey?" said Mal, glancing at me.

Stacey looked up, her blue eyes misting over. "He *broke up* with me. Can you believe it?" (Mal's eyes widened.)

"Why? Did you two have a fight?" I asked.

"Of course not." She ran her hand very quickly over her eyes. "We never fight."

"Then what happened?"

She shrugged. "I can't figure it out. He just said that these past two weeks have been great, but that it's over. He wants to go home and date other people. He doesn't want to be tied up with me."

"Gosh," said Mal breathily.

I thought guiltily of Logan. "But couldn't you date other people and still stay in touch with each other?"

Stacey shook her head. "He doesn't see it that way." She stood up and leaned against

118

the railing. "You're really lucky you have Logan waiting for you back home, Mary Anne. As you always say, he's your one true love."

Oh, yes. I had been saying that, hadn't I?

Stacey gave a long sigh. "It must be nice to have someone to count on."

Mal looked from Stacey to me with interest. She's just beginning to think that not all boys are jerks.

Margo and Claire came out on the porch then, so the conversation was over, but I couldn't stop thinking about Logan and Alex and how confused I was. Whenever I was with Alex, I had a wonderful time. Maybe I was even in love with him. I wasn't sure. And when I thought of Logan — that sweet smile, that deep voice — I thought I was in love with *him!* You can't be in love with two boys at once, can you? I just didn't know.

Alex and I decided to spend our last night together at the "real" restaurant, since we had had so much fun there before. As it turned out, it was a big mistake. Everything seemed different this time, and I couldn't put my finger on it.

For one thing, Alex had absolutely nothing to say. Naturally that made me very nervous, and when I get nervous I clam up. So both of us were sitting there like ventriloquist dummies, waiting for someone to make us talk.

I *had* to break the silence or I would go crazy, so I made a big deal out of choosing dinner. "Let's do something wild and *not* order fish," I said gaily. "That's the rule tonight. You can order anything but fish or shellfish."

Alex smiled politely. He must have thought I was crazy. "Whatever you say." He glanced at the menu. "There won't be much of a choice, though. After all, this *is* a seafood restaurant."

"Oh, there will be enough to choose from. It will just be a challenge." I tried a little laugh that didn't quite come off. Why had I started this?

"I suppose we could try the spaghetti." Alex smiled, but his heart wasn't in it.

"No way," I said. I shook my finger at him. "It has clam sauce."

"Oh, sorry." He stared at the menu for a long time. "Well," he said finally, "we could try the giant sub sandwich. I'm sure that doesn't have any fish in it."

"Sounds good to me!" I laughed like I was having the time of my life. When the sandwich arrived, I felt like crawling under the table. In the first place you should never order a sub sandwich when you're eating out because they are incredibly messy. Tomato slices slide down your chin, mayonnaise squirts out of both ends, and salami slithers into your lap. Not a pretty sight. In the second place, they are *huge*. This sandwich looked bigger than my head. I realized too late that we should have split one between us.

The only good thing was that now we had an excuse not to talk. We were too busy working our way through a mountain of cold cuts and French bread. I told Alex a little more about the Pike kids, and he talked about his softball team, but somehow the conversation never got going. We weren't really talking, we were "saying lines," just like you do in a school play. Except it felt like we were doing *different* plays, because the lines didn't sound right.

I thought the meal would *never* end, and when it finally did, I reached for the check.

"You can't do that," Alex said, making a grab for it.

"Why not?"

"Girls don't pay for dates."

"Sure they do. Logan and I always take turns paying."

"Who's Logan?"

Uh-oh. "He's my, uh, boyfriend. Back home in Stoneybrook." The truth was finally out!

Alex didn't seem too upset. "I have a girl-friend back home, too," he said casually.

"That's nice," I said. What was I talking about?

"What is?"

"That you have a girlfriend. And I have a boyfriend."

Alex looked at me and burst out laughing. "What's so funny?" I asked.

"I can't believe we're having this conversation, can you?"

I started laughing. "Not really. It sure beats hearing about your pitching arm, though."

Alex laughed even harder then, and I knew that everything would be okay. Suddenly he was the warm, funny Alex I knew, and we talked until it was time to go. (He ended up letting me pay the check.)

Later on, when we walked along the board-walk, I thought about how much I liked Alex, and how much fun we had had at Sea City. We were pals — friends — and it was much nicer than being boyfriend and girlfriend. After all, we each *had* a romantic relationship back home. Why complicate things?

"You know what?" Alex said, walking me up the Pikes' porch steps. "This has been one of the best nights of my life."

"You know what? I feel exactly the same way!"

"Friends?" He leaned forward and gave me a big hug.

I nodded. "Forever."

Friday

Dear Dad and Sharon,

Sometimes kids are amazing! Vanessa surprised me by coming up with a very grown-up solution to a tough problem. I can't believe I'm going to see you and Dawn tomorrow before you even get this card! This vacation has been fun, but I can't wait to get home.

Love,
Mary Anne

Mr. and Mrs. Pike were sitting in the kitchen when I got home from my date with Alex.

"Did you have a good time?" Mrs. Pike asked.

"I had a *wonderful* time." We were speaking in low voices, because everyone else was in bed.

Mrs. Pike smiled. "Mmm, sounds serious," she said teasingly. "Maybe you better sit down and talk about it over a piece of apple pie."

I laughed. "No, that's the great part about it. It's not serious at all." I realized they had no idea what I was talking about and decided to leave it that way. "And thanks for the pie, but we had a big dinner, and I'm stuffed. I think I'll just go to bed."

"Sleep well," Mr. Pike said. "Tomorrow's a busy day."

I tiptoed up the stairs, suddenly very tired. I was all set to open my bedroom door when I saw a faint light at the end of the hall. It was coming from under the door to the room Mal and Vanessa were sharing. I decided to check on things.

"What's up?" I whispered, sticking my head in the door. Mallory was sound asleep, but Vanessa was sitting up in bed, her notepad balanced on her knees, a small reading light on.

She motioned me over to the bed. "I'm writing to Chris," she said quietly.

I sat down carefully on the edge of the bed. "What did you decide to tell him?"

"Well," she said, "I tried to look at the problem from every angle, and I figured out there was only one solution."

I was impressed with how grown-up she sounded. I had been thinking about the problem all day and didn't have a clue what to do. I was totally stumped.

She took a deep breath. "This is what I've come up with. Chris thinks Mal is his secret admirer."

"Right."

"And he wants to take her out Saturday night." She paused. "So the answer is obvious."

"It is?" I had no idea what she was going to say next.

"It's very simple. We won't *be* here Saturday night. We're leaving tomorrow. So all I have to do is write Chris another poem and tell him how disappointed I am that we'll be back in Stoneybrook."

"You're not going to tell him that *you*, and

not Mallory, were the one who fell in love with him and sent him those poems?"

She shook her head. "What good would it do? Mallory is the one he likes. This way is much better. He'll never know the real story, and neither will Mallory."

It was pretty hard to believe that a nine-year-old kid could come up with such a great idea.

"I'll read the poem to you if you like, but you've got to promise me something. If you think it's silly, please tell me. I don't want to make a *total* idiot of myself."

Just then, Mallory made a funny snuffling noise in her sleep and rolled over. Vanessa and I froze for a minute and then relaxed. "It's okay. She's a very heavy sleeper. She's just dreaming," said Vanessa.

"Read the poem," I whispered.

" 'Dear Chris,
I'd love to see you tonight,
but the timing just isn't right.
We're leaving Sea City today,
and going far away.
I'll always remember your smile,
please think of me once in a while.
I ♡ you forever, your secret admirer.' "

Vanessa's voice choked up a little on the last line, and I had a lump in my throat. "It's a beautiful poem," I told her. "You said just the right thing, and it's not silly at all."

"Are you sure?"

"I'm sure." I leaned over and hugged her. "I'm so proud of you, Vanessa. I know this must have been really hard to do."

"It was one of the hardest things I've done in my whole life." She hugged me very tightly, and I knew she was trying not to cry. "Will you help me deliver it to Ice-Cream Palace tomorrow?"

"Of course I will." I could barely get the words out because I had started to cry myself. All I need is to see someone sad or in trouble, and I immediately start bawling.

"Don't cry, Mary Anne," Vanessa whispered against my shoulder. That only made things worse, and before you know it, both of us were crying.

"I better go to my room," I said finally. "You need to get some sleep."

"Okay," she said, turning off the light and snuggling under the covers. She managed to smile at me, even though she looked a little weepy. "Thanks for helping me out."

"Any time." I headed for the door when a noise made me turn around suddenly.

"I told you I want sunscreen, not sunblock!" Mallory was sitting straight up in bed, pointing a finger at me. I felt like a criminal.

My heart stopped. "What — what did you say?" I stammered. I looked at Vanessa, who flipped the light back on. I knew my face must be flaming red.

"Lie down, Mallory. You're in the middle of a dream," Vanessa said calmly.

I was amazed. "She is? She looks like she's wide awake."

Vanessa nodded. "She does this all the time. She's sound asleep but she talks to herself. It's pretty creepy, but I'm used to it by now."

Vanessa hopped out of bed and gently pushed Mallory's shoulders until she was lying down again. Mallory's eyelids fluttered a few times and then closed.

Vanessa smiled as she got back in bed. "She won't remember a word of this in the morning," she said, as I tiptoed out of the room.

I was dying to crawl into bed, but there was one more hurdle to cross. Stacey. She was in bed, but she wasn't asleep. In fact, she was sitting up with a book. She closed it when I came in our bedroom, though.

"I'm glad you're back," she said. "I've been waiting up for you."

I felt bone-tired. "Look, Stacey," I said

wearily, "if you're all set for another argument, it will have to wait till morning." Stacey had seemed saner — almost nice — earlier in the evening, but I still didn't trust her. People who've been dumped like to pick fights.

"No, I don't want to argue with you, Mary Anne." She hesitated. "Just the opposite. I've been such a jerk. I want to apologize for the lousy way I treated you."

I could feel tears welling up in my eyes. Oh, no. Not again! I thought.

"Do you think you can ever forgive me?" Stacey asked in a quavery voice.

"Of course I can," I told her. "But please don't say another word about it, or I'll start crying."

"Okay," she said, laughing a little. "I don't want you to turn on the waterworks or we'll be drowning in here." She quickly changed the subject. "How was your date tonight?"

"It was great." I could feel myself breaking into a grin. "Really a super night."

Stacey looked surprised. "No sad goodbyes?"

I shook my head. "No, everything was wonderful. Because I finally figured something out."

"You did?"

I nodded. "Alex is a good friend, but Logan

is my boyfriend. The love of my life," I added, blushing a little. "Once I figured that out, everything fell into place. I don't feel confused anymore."

Stacey leaned back against the pillows. "I'm glad things worked out for you."

"I'm sorry they didn't work out for you," I said, reaching for my pajamas.

Stacey sighed. "Well, at least it's been an interesting vacation. Never a dull moment."

"Never a dull moment," I repeated.

"You know what, Mary Anne? I think I'll be kind of glad to get back to Stoneybrook."

"Mmm, me, too." I pulled on my pajamas and fell into bed.

"Do you think Stoneybrook will seem dull after Sea City?"

I yawned and buried my head in the pillow. "No," I mumbled. "I think it will seem . . . peaceful." Stacey said something else, but I had already pulled the quilt over my shoulders and was heading for a dream.

CHAPTER 15

"Who has the beach blankets?"

"My bathing suit is still wet!"

"My inner tube has a leak."

"Good, it has to be deflated anyway."

Moving out of the Sea City house was just as hectic as moving in. Maybe more so. Let's face it, packing up to go home is never as much fun as unpacking in a new place. The excitement just isn't there. The house looked empty now that most of our belongings were stashed in the cars.

Mr. Pike was cooking an early breakfast, while I helped Mrs. Pike clean out the refrigerator.

"At least we don't have many leftovers," she said, tossing some cold cuts into a cooler. "How about the pantry?" she said to Stacey, who was opening cabinet doors all over the kitchen.

"It's almost bare," Stacey said. "So far all

I've found are some stale potato chips, a piece of bubble gum, and three Oreo cookies." She peered at something moving on one of the shelves. "Yuck! And a few ants."

"You don't have to pack those," Mr. Pike teased her.

All of the kids wanted to take a last swim after breakfast, but the sky was overcast, and they finally decided against it. I was glad. Now that our vacation was over, I was eager to get back to Stoneybrook. Of course I had one important thing to do before we left. I had to keep my promise to Vanessa to take her to Ice-Cream Palace.

"It would have been nice if the sun was shining on our last day here," Stacey said, sitting down to breakfast. "I could have used another hour on the backs of my legs."

"The backs of your legs look fine," Mal told her. Stacey had been aiming for the perfect tan for the past two weeks. She brought her watch to the beach and carefully turned over every half hour so her tan would be even. She reminded me of a chicken rotating on a barbecue grill, but I didn't tell her so. (I still looked as pale as ever, because I had worn my caftan and hat every single day.)

"Can we play on the beach before we go, Dad?" Adam asked.

"Yeah, let's build one more sand castle," Jordan chimed in.

Mr. Pike looked at Mrs. Pike. "I'll leave it up to you."

"Well, I don't know," Mrs. Pike began, "the swimsuits are packed now."

"We don't need our suits to play in the sand," Nicky said.

"You win." Mrs. Pike got up and started to clear the table. "I want to get going by eleven, though." She looked at Stacey and me. "We seem to have everything under control here. Is there anything you girls would like to do before we leave?"

"I think I'll play with the kids on the beach," Stacey said. "Who knows? Maybe you can get a tan on a cloudy day."

I caught up with Stacey as she was heading toward the porch. "There's something Vanessa and I have to do in town," I said quickly. "Can you and Mal handle things here while we're gone?"

"Sure." Stacey looked puzzled but didn't ask any questions.

I told Mrs. Pike that Vanessa wanted one last trip into town. Then I nodded to Vanessa, who was clutching her poem in her hand, and we headed for Ice-Cream Palace.

I was feeling a little nervous by this time,

134

but Vanessa was very cool as we walked along the boardwalk. I found out that she had planned everything down to the second.

"Slow up a little," she said. "I want to get there exactly at ten-fifteen."

"You do? What happens at ten-fifteen?"

"That's when the other boy behind the counter takes his break. Chris is really busy then because he has to handle all the customers himself."

I was amazed at the way she had thought things out. "What are we going to do exactly?"

She smiled. "You'll see."

We peered in the window just as a sandy-haired boy flung his cap on the counter and headed out the front door. Right on cue, a bunch of giggling girls barreled *into* Ice-Cream Palace and nearly collided with him.

"Perfect," Vanessa said under her breath. "Chris will go crazy trying to wait on all those kids at once."

She grabbed my hand, and we sneaked in behind the girls. Chris was facing us, scooping out ice cream. Vanessa hung back for a moment, staying out of sight. She waited until he turned around to use the whipped-cream machine, and then she darted forward to toss the note on the counter. Before I knew what had happened, the whole thing was over and we were outside.

Hearts pounding, we took a few steps and then stopped to hug each other. "We made it!" Vanessa cried.

"We made it," I echoed. I was glad to see she could smile about it.

Later that day, we were back in Stoneybrook. I was practically bouncing off the seat when Mrs. Pike pulled into my driveway.

"You did a great job, honey," Mrs. Pike said, handing me an envelope. I knew it contained a nice check, but that was the last thing on my mind. I wanted to run right inside and see everyone.

"Good-bye, Mary Anne!" shouted Stacey and the Pikes as I raced for the kitchen door.

When I burst into the kitchen, Sharon was standing at the sink. "Oh, I'm so glad you're back!" she said, giving me a big hug. "We really missed you."

"I missed you, too."

A moment later, Dad hurried in to hug me, with Tigger at his heels. "He's been meowing since you left," Dad said. "I think he was lonely."

I scooped up Tigger and cradled him in my arms. He started purring like a motorboat and

I knew he was happy to see me. And I was happy to be back. I looked around the kitchen as if I had never seen it before. Sea City had been fun, but it was great to be home.

"Where's Dawn?"

"She's upstairs lying down," Sharon said. "But she asked me to wake her up the minute you got back."

Dawn was napping in the middle of the day? "What's wrong? Is she sick?" I asked.

"She flew in from California yesterday and she has jet lag. She's been acting like a zombie. If you want to relax for a minute, I'll go get her."

I decided to make a quick phone call while I waited for Dawn to make her appearance. A moment later, Logan's warm voice came flowing through the phone wires.

"Hi, it's me," I said softly. I was trying to sound cool, but I couldn't keep the excitement out of my voice.

"You're back!" Logan exclaimed. He sounded *really* pleased, and I could feel myself grinning from ear to ear.

"I just got here."

"I missed you."

"Me, too," I assured him.

We made plans to see each other after dinner and said good-bye just as Dawn staggered down the stairs in her bathrobe. She looked like she had been awake for forty-eight hours. Her face was pale, her eyes were glazed over, and her long hair was lifeless. "Hi there," she said.

"Hi yourself." I put my arms around her and squeezed her tightly. "Are you sure you're okay?"

Dawn opened her mouth in a jaw-breaking yawn and then collapsed on the sofa. "I'm okay. I just feel like I want to sleep for a year."

"I'll make you girls some cinnamon-apple tea while you catch up on things," Sharon offered.

"That would be nice, Mom." Dawn yawned again. When we were alone, she tucked a pillow behind her head. "Okay," she said. "You go first. I want to hear *everything* about Sea City."

"Everything?"

"You can start by telling me about Alex. And Toby — is that the boy Stacey was going out with? And I want to hear what happened with Vanessa." Dawn had obviously paid close attention to the postcards I'd sent her.

"This is going to take awhile," I said, settling down on the floor. Tigger immediately jumped into my lap. "The problem is there were just so many boys. Things got so complicated."

"That's okay," Dawn said, waving her hand. "Start at the beginning and don't leave anything out. I'm not going anywhere."

I took a deep breath and plunged in. "It all started when we saw Alex and Toby on the beach. Or I should say, when they saw us. . . ."

Dawn and I talked until dinnertime, and afterward she sat on my bed while I unpacked.

"So you think Vanessa is over her broken heart?" she asked me.

"I'm sure of it. She handled it very well. I'm proud of her." I reached for a pile of T-shirts, and something white caught my eye. A piece of notebook paper was tucked between my shirts.

It was a poem from Vanessa, and my eyes misted over when I read it.

Dear Mary Anne,
  Love can hurt, love can sting,
  a broken heart can never sing.
  Boys will come, boys will go
  but a friend is forever, this I know.
  A friend is rare and hard to find
  everyone knows it's true.

You helped me through a very bad time
I'll always be grateful to you.
Thank you, Mary Anne.   Love, Vanessa

"Yes," I said softly. "I think Vanessa will be just fine."

Dear Reader,

In *Mary Anne and Too Many Boys*, Mary Anne finds herself torn between Logan and Alex. In the end, she realizes that Logan is the boy for her. Many kids write to me saying they are concerned because they don't have a boyfriend or girlfriend. While Mary Anne may be ready for a steady relationship, lots of kids her age are not! The truth is, many kids feel more comfortable being a friend instead of a boyfriend or girlfriend—like Mary Anne and Alex. Or Kristy and Bart. Sometimes knowing when you're ready for a relationship can be confusing. The most important thing is always to do what feels right for you.

Happy reading,

Ann M. Martin

L. GODWIN

Ann M. Martin

About the Author

ANN MATTHEWS MARTIN was born on August 12, 1955. She grew up in Princeton, NJ, with her parents and her younger sister, Jane.

Although Ann used to be a teacher and then an editor of children's books, she's now a full-time writer. She gets the ideas for her books from many different places. Some are based on personal experiences. Others are based on childhood memories and feelings. Many are written about contemporary problems or events.

All of Ann's characters, even the members of the Baby-sitters Club, are made up. (So is Stoneybrook.) But many of her characters are based on real people. Sometimes Ann names her characters after people she knows, other times she chooses names she likes.

In addition to the Baby-sitters Club books, Ann Martin has written many other books for children. Her favorite is *Ten Kids, No Pets* because she loves big families and she loves animals. Her favorite Baby-sitters Club book is *Kristy's Big Day*. (By the way, Kristy is her favorite baby-sitter!)

Ann M. Martin now lives in New York with her cats, Gussie and Woody. Her hobbies are reading, sewing, and needlework — especially making clothes for children.

Notebook Pages

This Baby-sitters Club book belongs to _____ .

I am _____ years old and in the _____

grade.

The name of my school is _____ .

I got this BSC book from _____ .

I started reading it on _____ and

finished reading it on _____ .

The place where I read most of this book is _____ .

My favorite part was when _____ .

If I could change anything in the story, it might be the part when

_____ .

My favorite character in the Baby-sitters Club is _____ .

The BSC member I am most like is _____

because _____ .

If I could write a Baby-sitters Club book it would be about ____

_____

#34 Mary Anne and Too Many Boys

When they return to Sea City, Mary Anne, Stacey, and Mal find too much trouble with too many boys! Mary Anne thinks she has to choose between Alex and Logan. If I were Mary Anne, I would have chosen _____ because _____ _____ _____. In fact, if I had to choose a character to go out with, it would be _____ because _____ _____. If I were Toby or Alex, the baby-sitter I would most want to go out with would be _____ _____ because _____ _____. One of the problems with too many boys is that Vanessa's heart is broken by Chris. Someone who once broke my heart is _____ _____ because _____ _____. In the end, Vanessa recovers and Mary Anne decides that she and Alex will just be friends. One person I am better off as friends with is _____.

MARY ANNE'S

Party girl -- age 4

Sitting for the Pikes is always an adventure.

Sitting for Andrea and Jenny Prezzioso -- a quiet moment.

SCRAPBOOK

Logan and me.
Summer luv at Sea City.

My family...
Jeff, Dad and Sharon
Dawn and me and Tigger

Illustrations by Angelo Tillery

Read all the books
about **Mary Anne**
in the Baby-sitters Club series
by Ann M. Martin

THE BABY-SITTERS CLUB®

The best friends you'll ever have!

Collect 'em all!

by Ann M. Martin

☐ MG43388-1	#1	Kristy's Great Idea	$3.50
☐ MG43387-3	#10	Logan Likes Mary Anne!	$3.99
☐ MG43717-8	#15	Little Miss Stoneybrook...and Dawn	$3.50
☐ MG43722-4	#20	Kristy and the Walking Disaster	$3.50
☐ MG43347-4	#25	Mary Anne and the Search for Tigger	$3.50
☐ MG42498-X	#30	Mary Anne and the Great Romance	$3.50
☐ MG42508-0	#35	Stacey and the Mystery of Stoneybrook	$3.50
☐ MG44082-9	#40	Claudia and the Middle School Mystery	$3.25
☐ MG43574-4	#45	Kristy and the Baby Parade	$3.50
☐ MG44969-9	#50	Dawn's Big Date	$3.50
☐ MG44968-0	#51	Stacey's Ex-Best Friend	$3.50
☐ MG44966-4	#52	Mary Anne + 2 Many Babies	$3.50
☐ MG44967-2	#53	Kristy for President	$3.25
☐ MG44965-6	#54	Mallory and the Dream Horse	$3.25
☐ MG44964-8	#55	Jessi's Gold Medal	$3.25
☐ MG45657-1	#56	Keep Out, Claudia!	$3.50
☐ MG45658-X	#57	Dawn Saves the Planet	$3.50
☐ MG45659-8	#58	Stacey's Choice	$3.50
☐ MG45660-1	#59	Mallory Hates Boys (and Gym)	$3.50
☐ MG45662-8	#60	Mary Anne's Makeover	$3.50
☐ MG45663-6	#61	Jessi's and the Awful Secret	$3.50
☐ MG45664-4	#62	Kristy and the Worst Kid Ever	$3.50
☐ MG45665-2	#63	Claudia's Special Friend	$3.50
☐ MG45666-0	#64	Dawn's Family Feud	$3.50
☐ MG45667-9	#65	Stacey's Big Crush	$3.50
☐ MG47004-3	#66	Maid Mary Anne	$3.50
☐ MG47005-1	#67	Dawn's Big Move	$3.50
☐ MG47006-X	#68	Jessi and the Bad Baby-sitter	$3.50
☐ MG47007-8	#69	Get Well Soon, Mallory!	$3.50
☐ MG47008-6	#70	Stacey and the Cheerleaders	$3.50
☐ MG47009-4	#71	Claudia and the Perfect Boy	$3.50
☐ MG47010-8	#72	Dawn and the We Love Kids Club	$3.50
☐ MG47011-6	#73	Mary Anne and Miss Priss	$3.50
☐ MG47012-4	#74	Kristy and the Copycat	$3.50
☐ MG47013-2	#75	Jessi's Horrible Prank	$3.50
☐ MG47014-0	#76	Stacey's Lie	$3.50
☐ MG48221-1	#77	Dawn and Whitney, Friends Forever	$3.50

More titles... ➤

The Baby-sitters Club titles continued...

☐ MG48222-X	#78	**Claudia and the Crazy Peaches**	**$3.50**
☐ MG48223-8	#79	**Mary Anne Breaks the Rules**	**$3.50**
☐ MG48224-6	#80	**Mallory Pike, #1 Fan**	**$3.50**
☐ MG48225-4	#81	**Kristy and Mr. Mom**	**$3.50**
☐ MG48226-2	#82	**Jessi and the Troublemaker**	**$3.50**
☐ MG48235-1	#83	**Stacey vs. the BSC**	**$3.50**
☐ MG48228-9	#84	**Dawn and the School Spirit War**	**$3.50**
☐ MG48236-X	#85	**Claudi Kishli, Live from WSTO**	**$3.50**
☐ MG48227-0	#86	**Mary Anne and Camp BSC**	**$3.50**
☐ MG48237-8	#87	**Stacey and the Bad Girls**	**$3.50**
☐ MG22872-2	#88	**Farewell, Dawn**	**$3.50**
☐ MG22873-0	#89	**Kristy and the Dirty Diapers**	**$3.50**
☐ MG22874-9	#90	**Welcome to the BSC, Abby**	**$3.50**
☐ MG22875-1	#91	**Claudia and the First Thanksgiving**	**$3.50**
☐ MG22876-5	#92	**Mallory's Christmas Wish**	**$3.50**
☐ MG22877-3	#93	**Mary Anne and the Memory Garden**	**$3.99**
☐ MG22878-1	#94	**Stacey McGill, Super Sitter**	**$3.99**
☐ MG45575-3		**Logan's Story Special Edition Readers' Request**	**$3.25**
☐ MG47118-X		**Logan Bruno, Boy Baby-sitter** **Special Edition Readers' Request**	**$3.50**
☐ MG47756-0		**Shannon's Story Special Edition**	**$3.50**
☐ MG47686-6		**The Baby-sitters Club Guide to Baby-sitting**	**$3.25**
☐ MG47314-X		**The Baby-sitters Club Trivia and Puzzle Fun Book**	**$2.50**
☐ MG48400-1		**BSC Portrait Collection: Claudia's Book**	**$3.50**
☐ MG22864-1		**BSC Portrait Collection: Dawn's Book**	**$3.50**
☐ MG48399-4		**BSC Portrait Collection: Stacey's Book**	**$3.50**
☐ MG47151-1		**The Baby-sitters Club Chain Letter**	**$14.95**
☐ MG48295-5		**The Baby-sitters Club Secret Santa**	**$14.95**
☐ MG45074-3		**The Baby-sitters Club Notebook**	**$2.50**
☐ MG44783-1		**The Baby-sitters Club Postcard Book**	**$4.95**

Available wherever you buy books...or use this order form.

Scholastic Inc., P.O. Box 7502, 2931 E. McCarty Street, Jefferson City, MO 65102

Please send me the books I have checked above. I am enclosing $_____
(please add $2.00 to cover shipping and handling). Send check or money order—no cash or
C.O.D.s please.

Name _____ Birthdate_____

Address _____

City_____ State/Zip _____

Please allow four to six weeks for delivery. Offer good in the U.S. only. Sorry, mail orders are not available
to residents of Canada. Prices subject to change.

THE BABY-SITTERS CLUB®

by Ann M. Martin

Collect and read these exciting BSC Super Specials, Mysteries, and Super Mysteries along with your favorite Baby-sitters Club books!

BSC Super Specials

☐ BBK44240-6	Baby-sitters on Board! Super Special #1		$3.95
☐ BBK44239-2	Baby-sitters' Summer Vacation Super Special #2		$3.95
☐ BBK43973-1	Baby-sitters' Winter Vacation Super Special #3		$3.95
☐ BBK42493-9	Baby-sitters' Island Adventure Super Special #4		$3.95
☐ BBK43575-2	California Girls! Super Special #5		$3.95
☐ BBK43576-0	New York, New York! Super Special #6		$3.95
☐ BBK44963-X	Snowbound! Super Special #7		$3.95
☐ BBK44962-X	Baby-sitters at Shadow Lake Super Special #8		$3.95
☐ BBK45661-X	Starring The Baby-sitters Club! Super Special #9		$3.95
☐ BBK45674-1	Sea City, Here We Come! Super Special #10		$3.95
☐ BBK47015-9	The Baby-sitters Remember Super Special #11		$3.95
☐ BBK48308-0	Here Come the Bridesmaids! Super Special #12		$3.95

BSC Mysteries

☐ BAI44084-5	#1 Stacey and the Missing Ring	$3.50
☐ BAI44085-3	#2 Beware Dawn!	$3.50
☐ BAI44799-8	#3 Mallory and the Ghost Cat	$3.50
☐ BAI44800-5	#4 Kristy and the Missing Child	$3.50
☐ BAI44801-3	#5 Mary Anne and the Secret in the Attic	$3.50
☐ BAI44961-3	#6 The Mystery at Claudia's House	$3.50
☐ BAI44960-5	#7 Dawn and the Disappearing Dogs	$3.50
☐ BAI44959-1	#8 Jessi and the Jewel Thieves	$3.50
☐ BAI44958-3	#9 Kristy and the Haunted Mansion	$3.50

More titles ➡

The Baby-sitters Club books continued...

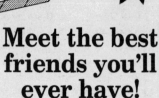

What's the scoop with Dawn, Kristy, Mallory, and the other girls?

Be the first to know with G★I★R★L★ magazine!

Hey, Baby-sitters Club readers! Now you can be the first on the block to get in on the action of G★I★R★L★ It's an exciting new magazine that lets you dig in and read...

★ Upcoming selections from Ann Martin's Baby-sitters Club books
★ Fun articles on handling stress, turning dreams into great careers, making and keeping best friends, and much more
★ Plus, all the latest on new movies, books, music, and sports!

To get in on the scoop, just cut and mail this coupon today. And don't forget to tell all your friends about G★I★R★L★ magazine!

A neat offer for you...6 issues for only $15.00.

Sign up today -- this special offer ends July 1, 1996!

❑ **YES!** Please send me G★I★R★L★ magazine. I will receive six fun-filled issues for only $15.00. Enclosed is a check (no cash, please) made payable to G★I★R★L★ for $15.00.

Just fill in, cut out, and mail this coupon with your payment of $15.00 to:
G★I★R★L★, c/o Scholastic Inc., 2931 East McCarty Street, Jefferson City, MO 65101.

Name _____

Address _____

City, State, ZIP _____

9013